Red CONSUMED

SUBSCRIBE LIVE LOVE BOOK 2

ALLYSON LINDT

For my eternal dragon

Chapter One

Wyatt wasn't surprised to see Parker standing next to Fiona, in the restaurant lobby. That didn't mean he was interested in hearing the sappy details of how the two of them finally climbed over the baggage that composed their past, to end up in a place where they were comfortable holding hands in public.

Fiona glared at Wyatt, her jaw set and a storm of irritation raging in her green eyes. "No." She spat the word out. "If you want to talk to me, you call me, like a normal person."

Fuck, she looked incredible. Even when she pointed that kind of venom at him, his body reacted without his permission, flames of need licking across his skin.

"If I'd done that, would you have taken my call?" Wyatt expected hostility. He wasn't sure how raw and open she'd be about it, but given he lied about not being her competition for a career-making contract—his career, specifically—seduced her, and literally fucked her while her best friend watched…

Her reaction was tame, all things considered.

She shook her head. "And you definitely don't set up a bullshit meeting, complete with a bullshit offer, to drag me into a public place and ambush me. Fuck you."

Inside the restaurant dining room, more heads turned toward them as her voice rose. He didn't mind the confrontation, but spilling the details for the world to hear wasn't on his list of ways this should go down.

"The meeting is sincere, the offer is real, and I didn't set this up." He kept his tone even and professional.

Parker gave a barking laugh. "Right. Because your company randomly decided they needed this app that happened to be created by the woman you were fucking."

He looked good too. Wyatt hated to admit that. He was pretty sure that, if Fiona was his Achilles Heel, Parker was the arrow that would kill him. Parker's demeanor had changed on camera in the past week. The dark shadows under his eyes faded, and his smile reached his eyes again.

He didn't talk about Fiona in his videos anymore, but Wyatt would bet money the shift coincided with her being back in his life.

"I don't suspect the decision was random, but it wasn't mine." Wyatt turned a pointed gaze on Parker. "Why are *you* here?"

"You expected me to come alone?" Fiona asked.

"Too easy." The innuendo slipped out before

Wyatt could stop it, and it summoned images of how enticing she looked when she climaxed.

She clenched her jaw. "Don't." At least she'd lowered her voice enough the diners weren't watching them anymore.

"Fine." He needed to yield somewhere, or this conversation wouldn't get them anywhere. "I hoped you'd leave the guard dog home. The two of you together are impossible." He hid a wince, as the confession slipped out. Impossible in the most tantalizing way, but only if they weren't pissed off at him.

Parker's smile was thin. "Tough shit."

Wyatt kept his focus on Fiona. "Can we be seated and talk?"

"No." She clipped off the response. "In fact, *we*—as in you and us—aren't doing anything. *We*—as in Parker and I—are leaving." She spun on her toe and pushed outside, Parker next to her, his arm around her waist.

Wyatt followed, a few feet back. "The offer is sincere. There really is a business proposal on the table." If she wasn't interested in talking about what happened between them, that was fine. He wasn't going to let her throw away a real opportunity, because of him. Especially since he tried to destroy her last one.

Fiona and Parker paused, and Parker turned. "So... she sucks you off, and she can have the contract?"

"Fuck you." *God*, this was getting old.

Parker smirked. "Not with a stolen dick."

"Is this a business meeting, or a playground

fight?" Wyatt struggled to hide his frustration.

Fiona turned to meet his gaze again. "You tell me."

"That's what I'm trying to do."

"I'm listening." She crossed her arms, pressing her breasts together and giving him a perfect view of the way her shirt hugged her torso. His attention drifted lower before he could stop it. She let out a tiny growl that did nothing to curb his sneaking arousal, and jammed her hands in her pockets.

He forced himself to look her in the eye. "The company is evaluating apps like yours. They found you without any input from me. The department making the purchasing decision doesn't have anything to do with me, beyond our offices being in the same building. If you go through this proposal process, I won't be involved."

"Then why are you here?" Parker asked.

"I saw Fiona's name on a budget request and called in a favor with the evaluating director. That's the one-hundred-percent, honest-to-God truth."

Fiona studied him, eyes narrowed and lips pursed. The deep furrow in Parker's brow and the way he clenched and unclenched his fist implied he was considering making good on the standing threat to deck Wyatt next time they met.

Fiona crossed the distance between them in a few quick strides, grabbed the lapels of Wyatt's jacket, and crushed her mouth to his.

His shock didn't stop his dick from hardening in an instant. *Fuck,* he missed this—her smooth lips, her faint scent, the tiny gasps she made when she was lost in the moment.

Wyatt reached out to pull her closer, and she stepped out of his grip. She slapped his hand away, and the sound echoed through the parking lot, while the sting rang through his wrist. He was glad she didn't do that to his face.

He pasted on a mask and removed all emotion from his voice. "Feel better?"

"Getting there."

"Can we talk now?"

"Business, yes. Everything else is off the table." Fiona matched his tone.

Wyatt was happy to make that concession for now. She could have walked away the moment she saw him. Asked to reschedule with the Draxon. Not kissed Wyatt. Told him *forget it*—she wasn't doing business with any company associated with him.

Instead, despite giving him grief, she was still here. And the way her kiss lingered on his lips, she wasn't completely Parker's.

Wyatt strode back to the restaurant entrance with them and held open the door. He wasn't sure what he hoped to accomplish, and going into this without a full-blown plan bothered him. He saw the bond between Parker and Fiona, and it was strong. One of those lust-, time-, and reason-defying connections.

And if anyone could sever it, he could.

Parker had to press his legs into his chair, to keep his knee from bouncing. The adrenaline racing through him ebbed slowly, leaving the gnawing in his stomach and prickling sensation under his skin.

He had half an ear on the conversation between Fiona and Wyatt. Enough to know it was actually business. The rest of his attention slid around the chaos living in his head.

The elation of making it to the next round of the competition.

The smug assurance every time Fiona squeezed his hand, which was muted by the scrape behind his ribs at the memory of watching her kiss Wyatt.

And the jealousy.

He expected that when it came to Fiona. Just because they were together didn't mean they'd worked past all their issues. But there was a twinge at knowing Wyatt was only here for her, and disappointed to see Parker, that was fucking with his head.

"We need to know you can handle that kind of stress and load," Wyatt said.

"As long as I get the appropriate warning, we're prepared for any size data package." Fiona's reply was smooth and professional.

Parker wanted to think it was his overactive imagination, hearing innuendo in a large part of what Wyatt and Fiona said, but he had a feeling they knew what they were saying. Underneath the entire exchange though, was the reality that this could be big for Fiona and Nick. Game-changer kind of stuff for their app. Parker wasn't going to ruin that for her.

They finished lunch and the meeting and strolled outside.

Wyatt shook Fiona's hand. "One of my colleagues will be in touch."

"Will you?" she asked. Her voice was devoid of

emotion.

Parker didn't hate hearing the question as much as he expected to.

Wyatt smirked. "I planned on it."

Parker wasn't opposed to that either, which he didn't understand at all.

"You need to call. I won't be so kind next time about being ambushed." There was no teasing in Fiona's voice. No room for negotiation.

Ambivalence raced through Parker, as he and Fiona walked away. "You can't do this with him if you're going to do business with this company," he said.

They wove through small groups of people, wandering around the outdoor mall.

"I'm not doing anything." The edge from telling Wyatt off was still in her voice. "And I know how to conduct myself with a client."

The last thing Parker wanted to do was turn this into an argument. "That's not what I meant." Sun warmed his face but didn't sear away the questions with no answers.

"It is, but I get it. Asking about him being in touch was a warning, not an offer."

So Parker *was* reading too much into things. "I'm still trying to figure out how this works." He kept the apology in his tone. It was easy in theory to accept that she was with him because she chose to be, even if she still had feelings for Wyatt. Seeing her deal with those feelings would take some adjusting. "I'm sorry."

"Me too. To both." She slipped her hand into his and pressed closer, resting her shoulder on his head as they walked down the street. "Let me make it up to you?"

The sugar and seduction in her voice turned his irritation to desire. "This is on him, not you. But if you had something in mind…"

"I'm sure we could come up with something you'd enjoy." She rested enough weight against him to steer him toward a shadowed alcove between shops. When they were out of the flow of traffic, she leaned back against the brick, watching him with her bottom lip caught between her teeth.

The playful smirk erased the negatives of the afternoon. He dipped his head to brush his lips over hers. "I enjoy a lot of things."

"Pick a couple. Or more." She hooked a finger in his waistband and tugged him closer.

Every inch of his body lit up like a live wire, as he pressed against her. The chatter of foot traffic drifted from a few feet away. A tiny whisper echoed in the back of his head, asking why sex with Fiona was tamer when Wyatt wasn't around.

She slid her hand lower, tracing the outline of his erection through his jeans and drawing him from semi-hard to painfully so.

He gripped her wrist and pulled her away from his cock, then grabbed her other hand and pinned her arms above her head. The giggle-squeal that tore from her throat was gasoline on the flames licking through his veins. He crushed his mouth to hers, devouring her groans and loving the way she ground her hip against his dick.

She was incredible, and he wasn't going to overanalyze things because she was playful and aggressive.

He nipped a line of bites up the side of her neck, to her ear. "You make me think you want to be pinned to the wall right now and fucked."

"It's tempting, isn't it?" Her soft question fell across his cheek.

Christ, it was. She was going to be the death of him. Or at least, a couple of days in jail for indecent exposure. And it would be worth it.

He glided his free hand under her shirt, using his body to block them from the view of casual passers-by. He cupped one breast and squeezed, as he dragged a thumb over her bra and the nipple underneath.

Her gasp rocketed through him. "More." Her plea was breathy.

He caught her earlobe between his teeth. "More what?"

"Finger-fuck me. Here. Please?"

The teasing, her recklessness—were they because they'd just walked away from Wyatt?

That was jealousy trying to rear its head again. Parker and Fiona hadn't been a couple long enough for him to have a feeling for the ebb and flow her moods when it came to sex.

And God damn it, if her words didn't unravel his control.

Chapter Two

Fiona didn't like humiliation without warning. She didn't like that seeing Wyatt bypassed her reason and overrode common sense. She *really* didn't like that she had someone amazing, and was risking him and everything they shared because she couldn't keep herself in check.

Parker teased his fingers under her jeans, while he devoured her moans.

She liked this. Feeling Parker. Falling into him. The thrill that came from what they were doing. The way he stood shielded them from anyone walking by, but only if people weren't paying attention.

He unhooked the button on her pants and dropped his hand under the lace of her panties. He lowered his head to her neck, to bite into the tender flesh where it met her shoulder. A fresh mark for a fresh day.

She gasped and arched her back, needing to get closer to his touch.

He skated his fingers along her folds, slipping

easily over her skin but not dipping between. Each new touch pushed away more of her confusion, replacing the thoughts with heady clouds.

The first few times she begged him for this teasing and playing in public, he spent too much time asking if she was sure.

There was no hesitation now—a lot of drawing things out and making her whimper. Her hips thrust toward his touch, and she strained against his grip on her wrists. Voices drifted in and out as people passed by a few feet away, unaware.

The pulse between her thighs grew stronger.

"Please?" She begged again.

His chuckle rumbled against her skin, and he dragged his mouth to a new spot on her shoulder. "I don't know…"

She loved this. The play. The risk. The lingering feeling of Wyatt's kiss under Parker's.

She shook the last thought away and focused more on Parker's touch. Need raced across her skin. Her senses danced with sparks of desire.

When he finally brushed over her clit, a mewl escaped her throat.

He raised his head to meet her gaze, diving into her soul. "*Fuck*, I love that sound." His voice was rough—delicious sandpaper gliding over tender nerves.

He pressed harder, tracing tiny circles around her sex. She'd already been close. The banter and tension at lunch were more tantalizing than she wanted to admit.

She tumbled into Parker's familiar touch. He knew how much weight to dig in and the right angle to use, and as she ground against his hand, orgasm flowed over her.

He didn't ease up until she broke from his grasp and grabbed his wrist. She watched his face as she pulled him free. Adoration and lust stared back at her from clear blue eyes.

Fiona sucked his fingers clean one at a time, enjoying his expression as much as the taste of herself on his skin.

"Better?" he asked, tone still gravelly.

She could still think—Wyatt's voice and scent and taste clogged her senses—and that was a problem. "Not yet, but close." She glanced around. At the sight of an ajar janitorial closet, inspiration spread through her, carried on the fading waves of climax.

"Over here." She tugged Parker into the small room and shut the door behind them.

"Red…" His warning was sharper in the dark.

She knew how to cut his restraints, and it would do the same for her. "I need to taste you." She was already undoing his jeans with one hand, and tracing his erection with the other.

His shaft was hot against her palm when she worked him free. The groan he let out sang to her soul. She trailed a nail down his chest, as she dropped to her knees.

"The floor has to be filthy in here." His protest was week.

"Good." She drew her thumb over the head of his cock, leaving a damp trail on the tender skin. He leaned his weight against the wall behind him.

The sharp tang of disinfectant stung her sinuses,

but it was muted by Parker's scent as she traced her tongue along his skin, then took him into her mouth.

His low moan seeped into her. The chill of of the concrete dug into her knees. This was what she wanted. What she needed.

She glided her mouth up and down, licking and sucking slowly, to tantalize.

The way he knotted his fingers in her hair, gripping tight and tugging her scalp, flipped a switch. Parker was losing himself in the sensations, and so could she.

He thrust against, cock diving deep, and she had to relax her throat, to keep from gagging on his length. The pace he set was fast and hard. Perfect. She focused on feeling. On pleasing him. The hint of salt on her tongue. His low, steady grunts. The delicious ache each time he pulled her hair, guiding her and holding her captive at the same time.

She adjusted her weight, to press her sex against the seam of her jeans. It wouldn't get her off, but riding that edge was its own pleasure.

"Fuck, Red, I'm so close."

She recognized the shift in his breathing. The faster thrusts, as he fucked her face. She stroked the tight skin of his balls, coaxing. The first spurt hit the back of her throat, followed by more.

She licked until he slowed to a stop, loosening the hold he had on her. As she pulled away, he slid from her mouth with a wet *slurp*.

Parker sank to the ground, hands finding her face in the dim light spilling under the door. The crush of his mouth against hers was as desperate as her desire to ignore her racing thoughts.

"God, you're amazing," he murmured into her lips.

Fiona smiled into another kiss, floating on euphoria.

He rested his forehead against hers. "And I wish I knew how to get him out of your head."

Pleasure fell away, and she stumbled off a mental cliff, back into reality. "I'm sorry." The apology slipped out before she could stop it. She was tired of having to say that. It was an admission, and at the same time, she hated that there was guilt associated with that feeling.

In so many ways, Parker's lack of reply was worse than the *so am I* she was used to.

♥♥♥

On a scale of *that was a mistake* to *sweet*, Wyatt rated the meeting with Fiona at about a *fuck yeah*.

He settled into the driver's seat of his car, then sent London a text.

Meeting went well. Tech looks solid to my untrained eye. They'd like to go on site, to get us a bid. I'll fill in the rest when we meet tomorrow.

He looked forward to seeing more of Fiona, but he'd remove himself from her bidding process going forward. The last thing he wanted was to ruin her chances at a solid opportunity. He'd feel that way even if he hadn't ripped the last one from her.

That didn't mean he'd steer clear of her. If she was going to visit their other offices, he had a feeling work might take him to the same places. He'd warn her before he bumped into her, though. Like he promised.

Wyatt's phone connected to his stereo when he started the BMW. He dialed into his work voicemail, and let it play as he drove back to the office. He'd listen to the messages again when he reached his destination, but this would give him an idea of what needed his attention and where his priorities fell.

There were a couple messages from his assistant, reminding him of appointments later today.

Another was from Brett, his former boss and now employee. Brett still wasn't happy about working for him. "I'm having some issues with the Grammie's contract. Can you give me a few minutes of your time today?"

Wyatt probably could. It was tempting to make the guy wait, but he wouldn't. Petty was fine for thoughts, but it didn't get work done.

"Hey." The greeting that spilled over the speakers turned Wyatt's blood to ice with a single syllable. "It's Devin."

Wyatt gripped the wheel until his knuckles ached. Devin was the ex-boyfriend who used Wyatt in a twisted, wingman sort of way, to help him pick up women, so Devin could stalk and assault several of them. Knowing he'd been part of that, even unwittingly, nauseated Wyatt.

"I left you a message a few weeks ago, but never heard back. I hope everything's all right." Devin's voice sent loathing and disgust racing through him. "Rumor is you've been promoted. Congratulations. Couldn't have happened to a more hyper-aggressive asshole."

Good to see you haven't changed either. The sarcasm helped Wyatt keep from snapping off a piece of the steering wheel.

"Anyway. I moved back to town recently, and I'd love to meet up. Not like we used to. I know you and I are in the past, but I'm hoping we can be friends. Give me a call and let me know when you're free." Devin left a number, then disconnected.

The inside of the car fell silent.

"Delete message." Wyatt sounded hollow to himself, and a ringing sank into his ears when he stopped talking.

Devin served five years in prison. It should have been longer, but even with Wyatt's testimony, only a couple of the charges stuck. Wyatt would be happy to see him castrated and forced to live out his days in some sort of dystopian human zoo.

How did someone go about hiring a hitman?

By the time he got back to the office, Wyatt had brought his mood back to even keel. That was the only way he'd get work done. He greeted his assistant and said he'd give Brett fifteen minutes if he could be here in the next five.

"I'll let him know."

"Thanks," Wyatt said and settled at his desk.

Less than two minutes later, Brett was seated across from him. "The Grammie's deal is falling apart."

"I doubt that." Wyatt was familiar with the other man's tendency to exaggerate. A month ago, it almost cost Wyatt his job. Now it was a simple task to gloss over it. "They signed a contract, the terms were clear, and your job is to make sure they understand and are happy with that."

Brett's glare could have shattered glass. "The

problem is they're demanding things that aren't in the contract. Things they say *you* promised them."

Wyatt hated working that sale. He could appreciate it led to meeting Fiona and Parker, though his betrayal gnawed at him. He'd also hated working with the self-important jackass who was his Grammie's contact. "I'm surprised you and Chuck don't get along like best pals."

"Did you promise him things that aren't in the contract?"

Wyatt met Brett's withering death glare with one of his own. "We discussed a number of topics. It was a sales pitch. You do remember how those work? I know better than to leave out details when the final contract is drawn up, though. What's he asking for?"

"Faster access to delivery drivers. Deliveries without uniforms or our branded vehicles."

"Things that were part of his negotiation with the other provider. Maybe he's confused about who promised him what."

Brett clenched his jaw. "That's helpful. He says your comment to him was that we'd do anything in our power to give him the same service and appearance he'd get from the competition, but with our corporate power driving it."

"I told him we'd see what we could do." Hence the month of business trips Wyatt took. Brett had threatened his job over those, too, until Wyatt landed the contract. "In the end, he came back to me and said he wasn't happy with our competition's offer. He dropped most of his requests, and he and I were on the same page when I handed him over to Contracts."

"He doesn't feel the same way."

"Then make him understand." Wyatt was done with this conversation. He'd severed ties with Chuck after the man insulted Fiona.

Brett stood, managing to make his chair scrape audibly across carpet. "Who knew? When you're in charge, you're even more asinine to deal with."

"Your fifteen minutes are up." Wyatt turned to his computer, to emphasize his point.

Brett left, but it didn't mean Wyatt cleared the conversation from his mind. The other man hadn't given up on trying to get Wyatt fired, and Wyatt's promotion was another reason for Brett to be pissed off.

Grammie's couldn't argue the details of the contract. Wyatt was better than that, but more critcally, his legal team excelled at their contracts.

That didn't stop him from being concerned that something he'd said to land the deal—and he'd said a lot—would come back to bite him in the ass.

Chapter Three

Parker had done too many live streams from hotel rooms in the last week. His vlog was supposed to be a video travel diary, and the closest his viewers were getting was a series of mass-manufactured flower prints, framed in gold and hanging behind him on one taupe wall after another.

"And thanks to all of you, I'm moving on to Month Three." He spoke to the webcam built into his laptop. "Thank you for each and every vote, view, and *Like*. Let's all do this together." *Someplace else.*

Atlanta was fine, but he rarely filmed in a single spot for more than a couple of days, and they'd been here a week.

He signed off and shut down the stream, before closing the lid on his computer. Fiona's voice drifted in from the other room. The separate bedroom was a necessity with her here, because he kept any hint that she was with him off-camera.

Neither of them was interested in a repeat of what happened with Tim. Fiona had been stalked.

Kidnapped. And it could have been so much worse. Parker was keeping her close, but out of sight.

He joined her.

"So when are you landing?" She was on the phone with Nick. "Got it… No, it's not a big deal. I can stick around here a few more days…"

Parker was grateful she focused on her notes, because he couldn't hide his frown. This meant either sucking up the dwindling filming options here or moving to the next state without her.

A few days apart were better than the months they'd been looking at right after the incident with Tim. Parker was a big boy. He could stop pouting.

"Hey." Her cheerful greeting snapped his attention back to her. She'd disconnected and was watching him with a hesitant smile.

He dropped onto the mattress next to her. "Is Nick coming here?"

"Yup. We've been invited to pitch to the delivery company. They said he could dial in, but he wants to make an impression."

Of course he did. Where Fiona was the tech, Nick was the real salesman behind the app.

"Are you introducing him to Wyatt?" Parker didn't know how much, if anything, she'd told Nick about the physical side of what happened with Wyatt. However, Nick knew the guy had palled around with them across multiple cities, never bothering to mention who he worked for.

She pursed her lips. "Wyatt's not part of the pitch, so I admit his name didn't come up."

Parker needed to wrap his head around his emotions. On the one hand, he'd kept his feelings for

Fiona to himself for years. He was happy she felt the same way about him that he did about her, but he couldn't expect her to drop her old life because he confessed his love.

Then again, Wyatt wasn't part of her old life. How long would Parker stick around if she couldn't make up her mind? "I'm heading out to that local sandwich place to do filming. Do you want dinner?"

Her smile whispered back in. "Sure."

He'd gotten good at keeping her off camera, but he would prerecord this trip instead of livestreaming it, like he did with any footage when she was around, so he could edit her out just in case. Parker wouldn't push the Wyatt issue now. She was being honest with him, and he didn't want to lose that. They hadn't been together long enough for him to expect her to move on.

He'd stop overanalyzing for now, and they'd cross the Wyatt bridge when they got there.

They chatted about random things, as they took a bus to the diner. Fiona relaxed, and Parker pushed Wyatt to the back of his mind.

When they arrived, Betty, the diner owner, welcomed him with a broad grin and outstretched arms. "I've got a table for you right over here. Have a seat and tell me what you'd like. The five-pound burger is free if you eat it in a single sitting." She looked them over. "But I don't imagine the two of you together eat that much in a day." Her tone was warm.

"Thanks," Parker said, as he and Fiona followed her across the room. "Before I turn on the camera, I want to go over a few things with you."

"Ah. Not filming yet." Betty's expression slipped a little.

"No. I always like to go over what to expect, get a release signed—things like that." Usually he handled the *what to expect* talk over the phone, but when he'd called to schedule, she had to run before he reached that point.

"Sure." She was still friendly, but some of the twang vanished from her voice, and she wasn't speaking as loudly.

Parker explained the process to her, including the release form. He also asked that she try to avoid standing near Fiona or addressing her while the camera was on, even though it might seem odd. It could be edited later, but he'd rather not have to cut something good because of that.

Betty nodded. "I understand. After you reached out to me, I did some looking into this competition, which led me to the stories about the kidnapping."

Fiona tightened her grip on his thigh. He gave her a reassuring squeeze. There were still rumors that the two of them invented the entire thing with Tim. That they faked Fiona's situation, to get Parker more views and sympathy.

"I believe you, hon." Betty was kind. "I can't imagine what you've been through, but having to defend yourself on top of it isn't right. I'm glad you're getting back out there again, though."

"Thanks." Fiona relaxed a little.

"You must be relieved at the news," Betty said.

Parker looked at Fiona. Her knitted eyebrows said she didn't have any more of an idea than he did what the *news* was.

"This Tim guy was remanded without bail, just a few hours ago. His history made him a flight risk," Betty said.

"Thank God." Fiona's relief was audible.

Betty patted her other hand. "I'll try to avoid getting you in the shot. Should we do this?"

"Let's." Parker set up one camera on a tripod, to capture the food. He had a second one he could keep mobile.

Betty launched into the same greeting she'd given when they arrived. They decided not to go for the five-pound burger, but did try the house specialty peach pie.

Parker followed Betty around the diner, getting footage of the kitchen and the cooking, and talking to some of the staff, but he turned off the camera while they ate, so he could enjoy Fiona's company.

He did a little more filming after the meal—a bit of wrap-up and some closing shots—before he put away his equipment.

He and Fiona were chatting with Betty, when a random guy dropped into the chair next to Fiona. "I know you." He didn't wait for a pause in the conversation. "You're one of those YouTube contest guys."

"I am." Normally Parker appreciated when someone recognized him. Random's approach and posture put him on edge, though.

"Does it ever bother you that you can't hold a candle to Ms. Passion?"

"Can't say I spend a lot of time thinking about it." Parker had to force himself not to speak through his teeth. Ms. Passion was a fellow contestant. She'd figured out how to review sex toys in a way that let her skirt censorship, and she was one of Fiona's most vocal detractors.

"I can't believe you two set that Tim guy up to take the fall for the sake of your cheap gimmick."

Parker clenched his fist, but Betty was on her feet before he could react. "I need to ask you to go." The southern hospitality was gone, replaced with a low, threatening tone.

Fiona covered Parker's hand. "Leave it, please," she whispered. The request barely drilled through his growing irritation.

"I'm out." Random stood and held up his hands. He stepped back from the table. "That won't change the fact that your girlfriend is a cheap whore who's destroying people's lives for your shit—"

Parker punched him in the face. *Fuck*, that hurt. He flexed his fingers. He must have hit bone.

Random swung back. The next few minutes were a blur of pain, shouting, and someone— multiple someones?—restraining them both.

One of the waitresses fetched him an ice pack that he held pressed to his face with handcuffed hands, in the back of the police car, as they took him to the station.

Betty asked the same waitress to give Fiona a ride and meet him there.

Three hours later, Parker still waited in Booking. He'd given up on alternating the bag of what was now water between his cheek and his knuckles. He might be crawling out of his head, if Fiona weren't next to him, resting her head against his arm.

"Do you want me to track you down more ice?" she asked.

"I'm all right."

She'd thanked him several times for defending her honor, and professed he was her hero. That almost made the pain worth it. Seeing her relaxed definitely did.

After an encounter like that, there was no way he was leaving her, even for a couple of days, to head to another city. He'd stick it out here for filming a little longer. Maybe Betty could refer him to a couple more places and put in a good word for him.

An officer with a clipboard stopped in front of them. "Parker Carney?"

"That's me."

"The other guy isn't pressing charges. You're free to go."

"What? Already? Thanks." He couldn't keep the sarcasm from his voice.

The cop raised his eyebrows. "Don't push your luck."

"Thank you. We appreciate it." Fiona tugged Parker to his feet and toward the exit before the conversation could go further.

She grabbed them a cab. The ride back to the hotel was mostly quiet, but she stayed close the entire time. How had he justified doubting her?

When they got back to their room, she filled their ice bucket and made him a new cold compress. She knelt on the bed next to him and pressed it gently to his face.

"This is going to be an ugly bruise," she said. "I can cover it up for the camera, if you want."

"Nah. I'm going to wear it like a badge."

Her laugh lightened his sour mood. She kissed him on the cheek. "You're such a caveman—bragging about defending your woman."

"I think you like me brutish."

She intertwined her fingers with his. "I like you here." A hint of seriousness slid into her voice. "I'm glad you didn't spend the night in jail."

"Me too. Are you doing all right?"

"I'm good." She shifted on the mattress, so she could lay her head on his leg.

Parker trailed his fingers through her hair, brushing the red strands away from her face. He needed to remember they had this. The longer he and Fiona were together, the more likely they were to be distracted by pretty men and women. But he and she shared this connection. It was solid, and it was real, and it was based on friendship that had blossomed.

She found something to watch, but he only processed half of it. His face throbbed, but it was numb from the cold, so he set the ice pack aside.

His phone rang, and he picked it up to hit *Ignore*. When he saw Betty's name, he answered instead. "Hello."

"Hey. Are y'all okay?"

Fiona muted the TV and rolled onto her back to watch him.

"My face has seen better days, but we're good."

"I'm glad to hear it." Hesitation lined Betty's voice. "So… I hate to do this to you, but I have to ask you not to use that footage from today. Any of it."

Parker's heart sank. "Not a problem. That's your right. May I ask why?"

"Stories about that fist fight of yours are already spreading around here. I know why you did it, and I don't blame you, but I don't need that kind of gossip linked to my shop. Going viral is one thing, but not for the wrong reasons."

"I understand." He didn't want to. He wanted to shout and rage and tell her this was a stupid fucking mistake and he could make her business. But he wasn't that person, and he didn't believe it anyway. "I appreciate you being honest with me about it."

"Thanks, hon. Best of luck to both of you. 'Night." She disconnected.

Parker tossed his phone aside with a sigh. She wasn't the first person to refuse to work with him because of the negative publicity his channel carried, but he hadn't lost a whole day of filming to any of the others.

"I'm sorry," Fiona said.

"It's all right. I'll figure it out." Begging for new places to film was better than leaving her here alone while he moved on to the next city.

But if he didn't get some decent footage soon, he wasn't going to make it through another round of this competition.

Chapter Four

Fiona sat with Nick in the shipping company lobby, waiting for someone to fetch them for their sales pitch. Her phone chimed. She winced as she grabbed for it.

"Sorry. I thought I turned it off," she said in response to Nick's scowl. She swiped the text message out of habit, and her pulse hammered in her ears when she saw it was from Wyatt.

Heard you're in the building today. No more surprise visits from me. Give me ten minutes after you're done?

"Everything all right?" Nick asked.

"Peachy." Fiona told herself to calm down. This wasn't worth getting worked up over, and definitely didn't deserve the flush of heat that raced through her.

I'm here with Nick, she replied.

Wyatt's response only took a few seconds. *Love to say hi to him, too. I just want to talk. Tell me no, and I won't bother you again.*

That would certainly be a solution. Her gut tightened at the thought. From most guys, she'd think *I won't bother you again* was a bluff. However, this gnawing was because she believed Wyatt when he said it. Was she ready to cut him off? The answer should be that of course she was.

A man about her age stopped in front of her and Nick. He was dressed smartly, in a suit and tie. "We're ready for you," he said.

Nick nudged her and stood. "We're all set. Aren't we?"

"Of course." Fiona followed. As they walked, she swiped a quick, *If I have time*, then set her phone to silent and dropped it in her purse.

She could picture vividly Wyatt's smirk at her lack of a *No*. Instead of the guilt she should feel, a pleasant tingle hummed inside, carried on whispers of what else she'd seen connected to that delicious smugness.

Fiona stashed the thoughts for later and stepped into the conference room with Nick.

Time to sell the hell out of their app.

Normally, she'd freeze in front of a room full of suits, but with Nick here, it was easy to let him do the talking, unless there were technical questions. She was glad he decided to make the trip, rather than dial in. They bounced well off each other when it came to work. And most things, when she thought about it.

There were concerns to address, and she expected that. The app was small—could it scale to meet demands? Nick gave them the publicly-known information about his most recent investor and business partner. That the funding allowed him and Fiona to bring on more staff.

He was honest about the time it took to upscale and train people, but promised to keep the shipping company in the loop as that changed.

As things wound down, London Draxon—the man Fiona *would* have met with the other day, if not for Wyatt—spoke up. "What's your schedule like over the next few days, Ms. Walters?"

"I'm afraid you'll have to be more specific." Fiona's smile was professional.

"Of course. I'd like you to go on site with our Louisiana call center, to get an idea of how they'll use the software, before you provide a final bid. Is that something you can do?"

Parker would be so happy to get out of this city and go anywhere else. "Of course. Now seems like as good a time as any to get everyone used to us working together." It was a presumptuous statement, but since she would provide the install and training support if the shipping company decided to sign the contract, she wanted to put the idea that she was accommodating in their heads.

There were a few more basic questions, but the meeting seemed to mostly be finished. As she and Nick shook everyone's hands, impulse raced through Fiona. She should ignore it, but the chanting of *do it* in her head wouldn't be silenced.

"Do you know if Wyatt Lindberg is in the office today?" she asked London. "I'd like to stop by and thank him for taking your place at lunch the other day, and making sure I stayed in touch with you."

"I think he is. If you want to wait in the lobby,

I'll have someone check and come get you."

"Thank you." Fiona's smile turned warm.

She and Nick headed back to their seats in the waiting area. "What are you doing?" he hissed.

"Exactly what I told him." Fiona kept her voice low.

"You neglected to mention to me that Wyatt was your lunch date."

She hadn't told Nick much about what happened on the trip. All he knew was that Wyatt appeared on one of Parker's videos and probably didn't have the best of intentions, since he hadn't told Fiona and Parker who he was.

"Does it matter?" she asked.

"*Yes.*" Nick stared at her with disbelief.

The same man who escorted them into the meeting interrupted the conversation. "Wyatt's available. He said to come on up. I'll show you where his office is."

She gave Nick a pointed glare. "It doesn't matter. End of story. I'll be back in ten minutes."

He snarled but wouldn't make a scene in a potential client's office. She was counting on that and grateful for it.

Her heart hammered against her ribs so loudly on the elevator ride up, she was surprised the assistant didn't glare at her. Why was she doing this?

Stupid question. Because Wyatt was a drug, and she didn't want him out of her system. As she stepped into his office, the dark wood furniture, full length window with a northern view, and bookcases lining the wall next to him were reminders of what he'd been willing to do to her, to earn this place.

That muted her desire. "Nice office." She kept her tone cool.

He stepped past her to close the door, brushing close enough she felt his heat. If she closed her eyes, she could sink into his tempting scent. She wouldn't do that, though.

"Thanks." His voice was deep and seductive in her ear. "Do I get another kiss? You're welcome to slap me after."

Arrogant fucking asshole. It didn't stop her from wanting him. She crossed her arms and put some distance between them. "You have nine minutes."

He returned to his side of the desk and sat, gesturing for her to do the same. "You do like your counting."

"Numbers don't lie." She perched on the edge of her chair. She wouldn't get comfortable, because she didn't trust herself not to let down her guard.

"I disagree. Are you going to tell Parker you came up to visit me?"

"Even if I don't, Nick will. He's waiting for me in the lobby. Eight minutes." The counting was as much for her benefit as his.

Wyatt's smile was casual and confident. "Eight and a half. I notice that wasn't a distinct *yes*, just like you give me a beautifully ambiguous answer each time I ask you a yes-or-no question about us."

"There's no *us*. How's that for unambiguous? Eight." Standing her ground was harder than she thought. She didn't want to push Wyatt away. Despite all the logical reasons she should—Parker and the fact that he'd betrayed her being at the top of the list—her body remembered. Being in this room, the private intimate space, glided over her with delicious temptation.

"Fine." The smoothness in his tone faltered. "I asked you up here so I could apologize. I never got a chance, and I can be more sincere without Parker interrupting. I'm sorry I kept things from you."

She glanced around the office. "Easy to say after the fact. You pretty much came out on top."

"On top? Really?" He twisted his mouth with amusement.

Damn it, she wanted those skilled lips on her. *Stop*. "You're a better man than rising to bad, unintended innuendo."

"You're killing me. Do I get any more sympathy with my apology if I tell you Grammie's is a pain in my ass now that we've signed them?"

She snorted a laugh. "Poor baby." She let the sarcasm slide into her retort. "I bet you don't even deal with them directly."

"I don't."

She stood. "Fantastic. You've apologized. I need to get back downstairs."

❤❤❤

Wyatt didn't want things to go this way, but Fiona was reacting better than should be expected. As in, she was still here. "Why did you come up?" he asked.

She worked her jaw, but no sound came out.

"You could have told me *no*. I would have respected that."

"And you could have let things go." She flicked

her tongue over her bottom lip.

Fuck, he missed doing that. "Do you want me to?"

She frowned.

"I don't," he said. "I'm stubborn. If you don't tell me to back the fuck off, I don't want to."

"I'm with Parker now."

This was an argument he could hold. "The two of you have been together for longer than I've known you, regardless of what you called it. I'm not trying to break you up." That was a lie. Then why didn't it feel like one? The contradiction bounced in his head, making his skull wince.

"I don't know what you want me to say." She sounded frustrated but not defensive.

"I want the truth. Give me that, and I'll let it go. You know I mean it." The biggest thing that drew him to and terrified him about Fiona was that she made it easy for him to tip his hand. He had no idea how he'd kept such a big secret from her for so long. "Did you hate me being there? Did you love it? Do you still crave it as desperately as I do?"

"Yes."

He didn't need clarification. She meant *all of the above*. "Finally. A straight answer."

"It doesn't change what you did, and I don't forgive you," she said.

"That's fair. Draxon has asked everyone bidding on this contract to pay a visit to our call center. Did he do the same with you?" It wasn't a complete change of subject, but it was the only thing he had left, to knock her off-balance.

"He did, and I will." She didn't falter.

Perfect. "Do you and Parker want a tour guide?"

"I'm pretty sure I'll have someone assigned, to show me the call center. If you mean around town, that's up to Parker."

It really wasn't. "If you want it, if you tell him I'll be there, he'll say *yes.*"

"I'm not going to do that to him."

"Parker didn't hate it any more than you did." And as much as he tried to argue otherwise, Wyatt liked having Parker there. Fiona was Wyatt's obsession, but Parker was a dangerous and delicious variable.

"He hates that I can't get you out of my head."

Wyatt refused to gloat over the confession. "I'll be there in two days. You know how to get a hold of me."

"No." Her sharp answer caught him off guard. "There's your answer. No, Wyatt."

She spun on her toe and walked out of the office.

Well, fucking hell. He didn't see that coming.

Chapter Five

Parker was wrapping up his current live stream, when he heard the lock on the hotel door *snick* open and someone push into the room. Time to sign off for the day.

"If I ask Parker, what will he tell me?" Nick's voice held an edge that implied he very much meant for it to carry into the next room.

Parker mentally rolled his eyes, but kept his composure for the camera. "The joys of hotel living, folks. As much as I'd like to let you listen to the neighbor's arguments—"

"And now you're silent? What the hell?" Nick said.

"—privacy and politeness win out over ratings today." Parker finished the thought as if he hadn't been interrupted. He gave the fastest version ever of his sign-off, then clicked *Stop*, to turn off the camera. He shut his laptop, to make sure the connection was severed, then yelled, "I'm done." There was no reason to keep the irritation out of his voice now.

"You haven't dropped this yet? Seriously?" Fiona strolled into the bedroom portion of the suite and hung her suit jacket up. "And since you forgot, the *Do Not Disturb* sign on the door means Parker's recording. If you're going to be an intolerable asshole, maybe at least care about not telling the world I'm here."

Nick, who was right behind her, went pale at the words. "I'm sorry."

This time Parker didn't hide his eyeroll. "At least you didn't use her name."

"I really am sorry," Nick said.

Too little, too late. Parker might not be so bothered if he hadn't heard Fiona warn Nick multiple times about the sign on the door. "I get it. What are you asking me about?"

"Nothing." Fiona set her shoes near her bag.

Nick scowled and leaned against the wall, blocking the doorway. "Who the fuck this Wyatt guy is."

Fantastic. Not.

"You already know who he is." Fiona's tone matched Parker's mental state. "For the fiftieth time, I went up to his office, to thank him for hooking us up with this meeting."

The new information might have rolled off Parker, but he was face-first in irritation. "Did you get another kiss while you were up there?"

The death glare Fiona shot him made him snap his jaw shut. *Shit.* She hadn't told Nick. Anything, he was guessing from the way Nick's eyes grew wide.

"Why would you kiss him?" Nick asked.

Fiona added a punctuated mouth twist to the

venomous look she was shooting Parker, and turned back to her brother. "Because, before we knew who he was, and before Parker and I were officially together, we met Wyatt, and he showed us more than some locals-only attractions in the cities we were in."

"I don't want to hear this, do I?" Nick crossed his arms, his posture going rigid.

"You insisted on the entire cab ride here that you did. Do you want details?" Fiona's hesitation was gone. "Do you want me to spell out how many different ways we experimented?"

Parker didn't want her to. His surface reaction was that he didn't care to relive the mistake, but something underneath insisted it was because it was private. For the three of them.

"No. *God* no." Nick looked horrified. "I don't want to hear about you sleeping around. *Experimenting*? Are you insane? With a stranger? There are so many issues with that, and... just... Who does that in real life? That's not normal."

A growl rolled through the room, and Parker realized it was him.

Hurt splashed across Fiona's face. "Don't be a prude," she told Nick.

"I'm not *being a prude*. I just don't want to think about you with two men. At once?" If Nick knew he was treading on thin ice and pissing them both off, it didn't seem to bother him. He looked at Parker. "And you're okay with that?"

"You know I'm bisexual, right?" Parker might have some concerns about his girlfriend being attracted to a lying, manipulative asshole, but he didn't appreciate the shade being cast on what they did with their private lives.

"That's not what I'm saying. You've loved her forever, and you're going to let her fuck another guy?"

"*Let* me? As if it's not my decision? And by the way, I'm still here, you know."

Parker looked at her. "I love you and trust you. You know that, and I don't care what *anyone* else says. I have to believe what we have is strong, and that you'll stay mine at the end of the day." The words felt solid and true as he said them. "Besides, it was pretty hot." He threw the last bit in to piss off Nick.

Fiona's smile shifted to a smirk.

Nick pushed away from the wall. "You two are insane. That's not love; it's fucked up. And if you're going to be insane, I don't want to hear about it, and I doubly don't want it to be such a raging, explicit, obviously dangerous conflict of interest."

"I think you missed the part of my life that makes it *mine* and keeps you from having a vote in my relationships. And even if you've suddenly turned into a possessive pig of a brother—"

"Someone stalked and kidnapped you." Nick's voice rose. "I'm allowed to be concerned."

"This isn't concern." Fiona's retort matched Parker's thoughts. "And I already told Wyatt *no*, we don't need him in our lives."

That was new. It sounded a lot more concrete than the way she left things at the end of lunch the other day.

"Good," Nick said.

Fiona narrowed her gaze. "Though you're

tempting me to call him back."

"Don't you dare," Nick ordered. "Don't ruin this business opportunity for us because you've got some nasty, disturbing kinks—"

"Stop." Parker was sick of this. "I think you need to go back to your room."

Nick turned his disbelief on Parker. "Talk some sense into your girlfriend."

"She's already sensible. Go back to your room before you say more things you'll regret."

Nick shook his head. "Un-fucking-believable. Fine." He turned on his toe and stormed from the room, the hotel door slamming shut behind him.

♥♥♥

Fury spilled through Fiona at her brother's words and was barely tempered by the fact that Parker never hesitated to take her side. She'd felt guilty about talking to Wyatt, but spite replaced that. She stared at the door Nick walked through. Did he think that little of the decisions she made and her ability to think for herself?

Maybe it was only this one thing that threw him off, but she'd never pegged him as closed minded before.

Parker wrapped his arms around her waist from behind and pressed his lips to the back of her neck. "I'm sorry." His words tingled against her skin.

"Me too." She leaned back into him, letting his touch chase away irrational thoughts. She needed to organize her brain better.

"How'd the meeting go otherwise?" Parker asked.

The change of topic was good. It would let her cool down. She spun to face him, not breaking his grip, and draped her arms around his neck. "I'm going to Houma, Louisiana, to check out their call center. Are you up for a change of scenery?"

"You know it. If Wyatt weren't so attached to this contract, I'd tell you to ask him if he'd show us around, just to piss Nick off."

Fiona wasn't going to call him on the lie. The tightening in her gut couldn't help but focus on how similar his suggestion was to Wyatt's. "If only."

"I'm sorry for spilling your secret."

"*Our* secret." She kept the teasing in her voice. "And it's okay. I've asked a lot of you, and you've given it to me without hesitation. You couldn't know."

"Do you want to open this relationship up?"

Fiona's brain stumbled on the new subject, and tripped on the question itself. "I... what?" The abruptness of his suggestion ached inside. He wanted to see other people? She didn't have a right to be wounded, but that didn't make the feeling go away. "Do you?"

"No." He brushed his lips over hers. "I mean, maybe? I don't know. It's not like I'm saying I want to take a break or see other people. I couldn't stand that."

"Okay." Relief trickled back in.

"But if you wanted to sometimes bring in a third person..."

The idea was enticing and bothersome at the same time. *This is more about Wyatt than a generic third body.* She swallowed the response, because it wasn't true. She was using Wyatt as an excuse to do what she enjoyed. Maybe it was time to stop casting that on him. "I'm not saying *no*, but I'm also not saying *yes*."

Parker gave a short laugh. "That's specific."

The sting of Nick's words still hummed under her skin, but Parker wasn't shaming her. This was the opposite, and she wanted to approach it that way. "I guess I'm not ruling it out, but I'm not interested in actively looking. I'd rather…" What?

"Rather what?"

She loved how on the same page they were today. "If we experiment, I'd rather it start with me and you."

"I'm fantastic with that." He dropped onto the edge of the mattress and pulled her down with him.

The result was a tangled mess and a bit of giggling, before they adjusted so she sat facing him, her legs tucked to one side.

"You have to tell me what you want, though," Parker said. "I guess we've never had that conversation."

Wyatt seemed to instinctively know. But that wasn't fair or reasonable. "Can I start with *a bit of everything*?"

"Probably not, but only because *everything* is a big list. We could do one-quarter of everything today, and fit the rest in tomorrow." Parker winked.

What should she say? There was an entire dungeon of fantasy tucked inside her thoughts, but she didn't know where to start. "It's too bad you had to lock in your channel description before the contest started."

"Why?"

"You could do travel reviews of the best hotels to have kinky sex in and the best positions for each one. Give Ms. Passion a run for her sex-toy affiliate code." Fiona liked the sound of that. Showing that woman up at her own *thing*.

"I don't think we draw the same crowd."

"No, but people do watch you for the sex appeal. I did." She traced a finger up his inner thigh, to emphasize her point.

He sucked in a sharp breath, as she drew higher. "Past tense?" he asked.

"Because I'm with you now. I get the full experience. Besides…" She trailed off as her mind caught up with what she was about to say. She needed to make sure it didn't come out as discouraging. "Your format has changed since I got here. You're more guarded. Less… flirty."

A frown shadowed across his face. "I do that for you."

She shook her head. "I don't want you to change the way you film, for me."

"Besides not mentioning you, making my filming locations match your work schedule—"

"*No.*" She didn't want this. This arrangement was supposed to make it possible for both of them to do what they loved. "The first doesn't have anything to do with how you talk to the camera. The second, I appreciate. I adore having you by my side so much, but if it's not working for you, don't blame me."

"It's not blame. It's a statement of fact. We've both changed since the contest began, and that's going to reflect in how I talk to the camera."

That wasn't the same as what he'd started saying, but she didn't want to pick a fight. The one with Nick was bad, but she was tired of arguing with Parker. "I still love the format and think your channel is awesome. And I'm not just saying that because I get to fuck the star of the show."

His smile no longer reached his eyes. "Thanks."

Turned out despondent Parker was almost as bad as argumentative. That sucked.

Chapter Six

Wyatt had to push, to finish his work at the call center in the morning. Even then, he didn't get out until after two. He'd already adjusted his schedule to be in town when Fiona was, and as he wrapped up for the day, he wished he hadn't.

He *knew* she'd take him up on his offer. Been so certain, he was willing to call in a couple of favors, to make sure he was here at the same time as her.

Now, he had to respect her *no*, and that meant working not to run into her. She made herself clear. He might be arrogant and aggressive, but he wouldn't stalk her. The stunt he pulled in Atlanta, placing himself as her lunch date, left a bad taste in his mouth.

He'd avoided her in the building today. Now he could grab a late lunch at a local place no one in the office ever went to, and then head back to his hotel, to work.

The short drive was pleasant. He loved this little suburb. This time of day, traffic wasn't bad, and the sandwich shop wouldn't be busy. It would give him time to sit and bullshit with the staff. That was always fun.

He was smiling by the time he reached his destination. As he pushed through the front door, a little bell chimed. So kitschy. So perfect.

"This was fantastic, thank you." A familiar voice drifted toward him, and he groaned inwardly. *Parker*.

Sure enough, he stood near the front counter, camera gear slung over one shoulder, as he chatted with the owner, Mike.

Wyatt could find another place for lunch. He turned to leave, and had his hand on the door, when he heard, "Are you kidding me with this?"

Busted. Which was ridiculous, because Wyatt was the opposite of *up to something*. He pasted on a pleasant mask and turned back to face Parker.

"How's it going?" Wyatt closed the distance between them, to keep the conversation quiet, in case it wasn't civil.

Parker snorted. "I can't believe you're here. Fiona told you *no*."

"Which is why I'm here, and not at the call center. If I wanted to follow Fiona, I'd put myself where she is, rather than going out of my way to be where she's not." Irritation crept into his tone.

Parker rolled his eyes. "So you happened to walk into the same place I was filming—"

"You've stopped announcing your schedule beforehand." Wyatt wasn't in the mood to be lectured. He wanted his lunch. "So if you're going to spin it that way, *you happened* to be filming in the place I always eat lunch when I'm in town."

Parker faltered. "I heard they make an incredible meatball sub here."

They did. It was the house specialty, and it was a mess to eat. Worth it, though. "And?"

"I wasn't disappointed."

"Hey." Mike interrupted, voice cheerful. "I didn't know you two were friends."

Wyatt clapped Parker on the shoulder. "Absolutely. We go way back. Can I get my usual, to go?" It wouldn't be the meatball sub. That didn't work well with white shirts and eating on a park bench. But he'd learned to make the hand-carved turkey yield.

Mike hollered Wyatt's order back to the kitchen, then turned back to him and Parker. "Up in five. Let me know if I can get either of you anything else." He returned to his work.

Wyatt pulled out a seat to wait, hiding his pleased surprise when Parker grabbed the chair across from him, spun it backwards, and straddled it.

Parker rested his arms on the back of the seat. "So maybe you know the place."

"Thanks for the consensus," Wyatt said dryly. Inspiration struck, and he almost felt like a cartoon character with a light bulb going on above his head. Could he work his way back into the couple's good graces through Parker? Maybe tearing them apart was a bad idea. "What's your afternoon look like?"

"Editing this footage. Trying to stay out of any fistfights. Praying to God this place doesn't change its mind about signing the release form."

The fistfight comment caught Wyatt's

attention, but before he could ask, Mike returned with his food. "On the house. As thanks for your friend's free advertising."

"Absolutely not." Wyatt plucked a twenty from his wallet. "Keep the change. But I'm glad you're working with Parker. I'm a huge fan of his show."

Mike grinned. "He's a nice guy, and who am I to turn down publicity? Besides, it was a lot of fun." He shook Parker's hand. "Catch you both around."

Wyatt grabbed the paper bag with his lunch and stood. "I'm going for a walk in the park, if you want to join me," he said to Parker.

"Not really." Parker fell into step beside him anyway. "Thanks for the good word." He sounded genuinely grateful.

Yeah, this could work. "I don't have to be in the office this afternoon. In fact, I'm trying to avoid it, for the previously mentioned redheaded reason. If you've got an hour or two, I'll give you the highlights tour of the town."

"Don't you want to eat?"

Wyatt nodded across the street. "We'll start there. I can point out a lot of from a bench."

"What's the catch?" Parker crossed the road with him.

"Why do you assume there's a catch?"

Parker gave a short laugh. "Gee, I wonder why I might not trust that your intentions are altruistic."

Wyatt brushed some loose grass from a wooden bench and made himself comfortable. "The longer I keep you talking, the more likely I am to find my way back into your lives." Sometimes honesty was the best deception. "And if it doesn't work, I have some company for the afternoon, regardless."

"It's not going to work, but I'll take the tour anyway."

"Perfect." This was what Wyatt needed.

Except, despite the confidence flowing through and out, he wondered if this was a mistake. He should let Fiona go. Trying to forget Fiona last time didn't work so well for him, but if she decided to take this to his bosses and complain about harassment, it would cost him his job. Besides, he was acting like an obsessed fucking puppy.

So why wasn't any of that enough to make him stop?

♥ ♥ ♥

Parker leaned back against the warm wood of the bench and enjoyed the heat of the sun on his face. It clashed with a gentle breeze and set the air at the perfect temperature.

He couldn't believe he was sitting with Wyatt, while the man ate lunch, and listening to a brief history of this town and some of its lesser-known attractions. The part of him that wanted to tell this guy to fuck off, again, was eerily silent.

It wasn't as if Parker had let his defenses down, though. Wyatt used him and Fiona, and if he was offering an olive branch in the form of help with filming—ulterior motives or not—Parker was going to take it.

This was also a chance to figure out what Fiona saw in Wyatt. Parker saw an arrogant man, who wasn't afraid to use people but managed to stay fucking sexy in the process.

And something about that drew Parker in. It was the same un-nameable quality that compelled him to accept any of Wyatt's invitations—the same thing that captured Parker's attention every time, however often he insisted to himself he was only putting up with Wyatt for Fiona's sake.

He was fascinated, and annoyed with himself and Wyatt because of it.

"About two miles south, there's a candy shop." Wyatt threw the bag holding the crumpled remnants of his lunch in the air and caught it. "They pull the taffy by hand. If you want, I can put you in touch with the manager."

Parker wanted to keep the *I'm so not interested* demeanor in place, but the conversation wasn't bad. He frowned when he realized how low the sun had fallen, and glanced at the clock on his phone. It was almost five. "Maybe. I'll think about it. I need to let Fiona know where I am." He sent her a quick text. Her reply came in a moment later. "She'll meet me here in about ten," he warned Wyatt.

"That's my cue to leave." Wyatt stood and tossed his garbage in the nearby can.

Parker stood too. "Thanks for the info. Seriously. It'll make a big difference."

"You know, if Fiona gets this contract, I'll be in a lot of the same places she will. If you want a tour guide…"

Parker expected this. Hell, Wyatt told him it was coming. Despite his annoyance, he couldn't help being impressed that Wyatt slid into the offer without hesitation. "I'm not going to take you up on that, because I respect Fiona's answer. But I am curious about you're so eager to help me out."

"I told you. I want to make amends for what I did. Believe it or not, I was being honest when I said I'm a fan of the show. I'm rooting for you."

Parker should let him go before Fiona arrived, but he needed a real answer. "I would have thought Ms. Passion would be more up your alley."

"She's got her pluses. I'm not a fan of the anti-Parker-and-Fiona rhetoric, though."

"So your offer is completely selfless." Parker pushed harder.

"Fuck no. I want to spend more time with Fiona. And for you to forgive me."

Considering a large part of Parker's issue with Wyatt was Fiona— "The two are a bit contradictory."

Wyatt shrugged and stepped closer, holding Parker's gaze. "It doesn't matter. I respect Fiona's *no.*" His tone had shifted, and something Parker couldn't identify mixed with the confidence. "Until she changes her mind. If you only want a list of places, I'll give them to you, and I'll put in a good word with the staff."

"And…?" Each time Parker thought he was about to get an answer, he was diverted again.

"And nothing."

"You're doing this out of the goodness of your heart?" Parker's irritation slipped through. He didn't like playing Wyatt's games. "You were willing to cost Fiona everything, until you face-planted in her pussy. And now you're going to give me this information and drop everything else?" The moment he said it, he knew he'd missed too much. *Until she changes her mind.*

He was an idiot. Wyatt was doing what he said he would, and Parker chose to brush that off? Because he thought was smart enough to avoid it?

Wyatt gave him that hungry-wolf grin. "I'm giving you the list, and then I'm waiting. I'll be in those cities, and in a week or three, *you're* going to call me."

"I will?" Parker had to force out the snort of disbelief. His mind insisted he wasn't that naive, but Wyatt's tone was compelling. And as wind swirled around them, Wyatt stood close. The scent of his cologne mingled with sunshine and flowed through Parker's senses.

If Fiona weren't in the picture, this would be a different scenario. Parker would yield, to see what this man would do. But she was, so it didn't matter.

"You will," Wyatt said. "Because the sex isn't the same when it's just the two of you, and she hasn't told you a quarter of the things she fantasizes about." The phoniness was gone, replaced by a low growl of conviction. "Public blow jobs will only sate curiosity for so long. Hers and yours. Besides, you won't be happy with monogamy. And I mean you, specifically."

"Bullshit." Parker was willing to listen to Wyatt's bravado to a point, but none of this was true. So why was he still here? Why didn't he turn and walk away and meet Fiona at the edge of the park?

Because desire compelled him to hear this out until the end. His pulse roared in his ears, and his nerve endings danced with need at how close Wyatt stood.

Wyatt searched his eyes, as if looking for evidence of exactly that. "Maybe it is. Maybe it's not. You've spent your adult life seeing the world and fucking who and when you want. Now you're done, because you have the woman of your dreams?"

"Yes." Because that was how relationships worked. And he'd imagined the waver in his own response.

"But you're thinking about what I'm saying, and you're wondering if I'm right." Wyatt stepped closer, his nose almost touching Parker's. "So you'll make her think it's all for her. *Call Wyatt, just this once. It's okay. We'll be okay.* And it will be, because you're curious too."

"Not about you, I'm not. I know what you are." Fuck this man, for climbing into his head, and fuck his own body, for reacting and betraying him. Indignation and lust raged in Parker. He clenched his jaw to keep them from spilling out.

"You don't know me any better than I know you. But I believe you know enough. And you want another taste anyway."

"Not all of us have a secret desire to be dominated." Parker wouldn't back down. He wouldn't be manipulated. And he definitely wouldn't give into the impulse to remember what it felt like to kiss Wyatt.

"It's true. You, for instance, want to explore. Watch. Play. Your suppressed desire is pleasure. You want more, and you keep denying yourself."

"I'm not denying anything." *Don't back off. Don't let him get under your skin.* Too late. Parker closed the last few centimeters between them and crushed his mouth to Wyatt's.

He saw the shock in Wyatt's eyes, but it morphed to satisfaction in a blink. That wouldn't make Parker pull away. He poured everything into the kiss—the fury, lust, and frustration.

Wyatt rested a hand at the back of his neck, holding him captive, and Parker didn't care. He devoured Wyatt's mouth, biting his lips. He ground against Wyatt's hard body.

The voice in the back of his head told him to stop, but that was the one thing he didn't have the desire for. Heat flooded through him, drawing his cock to life. Reminding him what else he loved about what he did.

Exploring.

He dropped a hand below Wyatt's waist, to cup his length through his trousers, and smirked against the kiss when Wyatt's erection jerked against his touch. The low growl—he didn't know whose it was—heated his blood further.

"Are you fucking kidding me with this?" Fiona's disbelief shattered the moment, and Parker's thoughts splintered into a million pieces.

Chapter Seven

Fiona didn't know who she was more furious with.

"Red, wait." Parker sprinted to her side and grabbed her arm.

She jerked free. Correction—she knew *exactly* who she was mad at. Wyatt didn't matter. The arrogant asshole probably planned to be here before she turned him down. But Parker...

She glared at him.

"Don't run off in a huff." Wyatt's request drew her attention.

She turned her ire on him. "Is this where you give me a bullshit story about how this was your doing, and not to blame him?" Why would she assume that? Oh, right. Because it didn't make sense, and it would throw her off balance. Whatever Wyatt was up to, he wouldn't be upfront about it.

"No. Definitely not. He kissed me," Wyatt said. "But last time you stormed away, things went downhill fast."

She cringed at the reminder and the whisper of concern under his smug words. "So make sure that doesn't happen again. Follow me. You've got a lot of practice."

Anger flashed in Wyatt's eyes, but something else lay underneath.

Fiona refused to think past the fury inside. She resumed walking toward the edge of the park.

Parker stepped in her path. "Hear me out, please?"

"Why?" The question was raw in her throat. "I'll apologize over and over again for the fact that—" She clamped her jaw shut, not willing to spill in front of Wyatt that she was struggling to move past him. "Everything we've talked about. And then you go and do this? After everything you've said?"

"I didn't— He was— He happened to walk into the same place I was filming, and we were talking," Parker said.

Fiona felt like her scowl was frozen in place. "Mouths and tongues were definitely involved."

"That was…" Parker frowned.

She raised her eyebrows, waiting for him to offer up some brilliant explanation.

"I was thinking he'd be a good tour guide, after all."

Fiona couldn't believe what she was hearing. "At least you more or less led with that. Like last time. You realize that despite your suggesting it, it's always been his idea."

Behind Parker, she saw Wyatt fighting a smirk. She pointed a narrow-eyed glare at him, and his face went blank.

"I do realize," Parker said. "And I also heard Nick."

"That's not making me any happier. Do you remember there's this big huge conflict-of-interest thing? Oh, and that you and I are a couple?" It was odd to approach this argument from the side Parker usually took. Except he didn't argue with her lingering infatuation. He was frustrated, but shouting wasn't his thing.

She never expected this was why he tolerated her crush. She didn't even know what *this* was that she'd walked in on.

Parker looked behind him, then back at her. "You don't have to leave with me, but can we talk without an audience?"

That was a good idea. She nodded, and they moved a few feet from Wyatt. A tiny part of her brain asked why they didn't go back to the hotel to talk. Or anywhere that Wyatt wasn't.

Because she didn't want to. If Parker wasn't pushing him away, she didn't have to either.

Wyatt lied to you.

So she wouldn't trust him. It was as easy as that. "What's going on?" she asked Parker, in a softer voice.

"He walked into the sandwich shop as I was wrapping up filming. Said he was trying to avoid you and didn't know I'd be there. I think he was telling the truth."

Fiona shrugged. It sounded plausible enough. "How do you get from there to groping him in the middle of the park?"

"He started talking, like he does, and I got

irritated, like I do…"

"So this was a dick-measuring contest, with a hands-on round?"

Parker pursed his lips. "I don't know what it was. Compulsion. Lust. Aggravation. And you're not the only one feeling the pull."

"Oh." Fiona's anger slipped. She tripped through highlights in her memories. Sure, Parker and Wyatt pushed each other, and watching them together sent tingles racing over her body, but the mutual distaste… Except it had faded. Right before they found out Wyatt lied, it was gone. Was her boyfriend infatuated with someone else? She didn't have any right to feel the ping in her chest, but she did.

Parker grasped her fingers, and she didn't pull away. "It's not like y—like I want to run away with the guy. He's slimy, but he's sexy. If you argue that, I'll know you're lying."

"I won't." She had too many thoughts and emotions tumbling through her head, to make sense of them. *Another chance.* The loud, insistent, nagging voice pointing out she could have both, for a little while. Get Wyatt out of her system.

"Besides"—Parker squeezed her hand gently—"maybe I can learn a few things from him."

"Like…?" The best angle for ass-slapping for maximum sting and minimum risk?

"How to relax in front of the camera again. How to shake off whatever's making me freeze up."

Right. Except Parker wasn't meeting her gaze. It was close, but it wasn't eye-contact.

"I'd like to see you happy with your views

again," she said. "Get back on track in the competition." And apparently, sex with the Big Bad Wolf was the way to do that.

"I hate to interrupt," Wyatt said, doing exactly that, "but if you two don't need me..."

Need was a strong word. *Want* was more appropriate.

Parker looked at him. "Where are your travels taking you next? I was wondering if you'd like to show me around town."

The corners of Wyatt's mouth twitched up in an unformed smile. "Probably North Carolina. We have an office near Beaufort, and I'm training some sales associates."

They were actually doing this. Fiona's mouth went dry, and her pulse hammered in her ears. Nick's voice nagged in her head, pointing out relationships didn't work this way. Bringing in a third person—who'd lied his way into their lives—wasn't spice; it was stupid.

Fortunately, she wasn't Nick. Despite his words and reason, she didn't want to see past the possibilities.

"We have to keep this discreet," she said. At least part of her brain was working.

Wyatt's smile emerged. "So I'm clear—I don't want any misunderstanding—you're not talking about the tour-guide part of things when you say *discreet*."

"I'm talking experimentation." Great. She couldn't bring herself to be an adult and say *sex*.

"We're talking about fucking." Parker didn't seem to have any issues with it. "Anything physical."

"Couldn't agree more," Wyatt said. "If Fiona gets this contract—and I'm going to breach protocol and tell her odds are good, because she's good, and I had nothing to do with that decision—getting caught is my ass as much as it is hers. This is just between the three of us."

The skip in her chest should have been at the confirmation she was probably about to secure this sale, but it wasn't. "This doesn't mean the past is forgiven, though. I don't trust you. Neither of us does."

Wyatt gritted his teeth and sucked in a breath through them. "That's not going to work for me."

Parker barked a laugh. "You expected otherwise?"

"Trust flows both ways. You don't trust me, you're more likely to betray me. If this gets out at all… we covered what happens."

"You haven't earned trust. If that's a deal breaker, the deal is broken." Fiona hated the taste of the words, but she did have some semblance of sanity left in her skull. "But like you said, exposure hurts me, too."

"Fine. I'll put it this way. If you want to *experiment*"—he looked at her—"you have to trust me. You have to do what I say and believe that I'm not trying to hurt you. Pain… maybe. That depends on you. But not betrayal."

The implication sent daggers of desire dancing along her nerves, and she swallowed the impulse to moan at the possibilities. "I'll give you everything in the bedroom, actual or metaphorical. Outside of that, you earn it."

"I'll take that for now." He looked at Parker. "You're okay with this?"

"I am."

She didn't know if she was bothered or relieved by Parker's lack of hesitation.

"Send me your itinerary. I'll rearrange filming to match," Parker said.

Wyatt nodded.

"We should get going." Parker tangled his fingers with Fiona's.

"Fiona. A moment." Wyatt's request stopped her. Again.

She both loathed and was compelled by how easily she reacted to his commands. She looked at him, lips pursed in expectation.

Parker squeezed her hand.

Wyatt moved close. She felt his heat through clothing. Saw the different-color flecks in his eyes. Smelled that tantalizing scent of cologne. He didn't touch her, but his gaze held hers. "Next time we see each other, I'm not going to hold back. I want to feel you again. Your tight pussy clenched around my cock. Your nails digging into my flesh, as you ride that edge of pleasure. And I won't play backup or be content to watch. Not next time. I'm going to mark you, so you remember. Make you scream until you're hoarse. Ensure you have trouble walking when I'm done. Do you have an issue with that?"

She'd protest, but she couldn't find her voice. Anticipation, hot and damp, pulsed between her legs. She bit her bottom lip, to hold back the *why wait?* "No," she said.

She swore she heard Parker's breathing quicken.

Wyatt smiled that same dangerous, devour-her smirk that always scrambled her thoughts. "Good."

Chapter Eight

Anticipation hummed over Wyatt's skin after he returned to his hotel. He'd spent his afternoon with Parker instead of working, and it turned out to be worth it. He'd have Fiona again. But that meant work still waited.

He wasn't fond of how Parker got under his skin, though. A simple kiss, and Wyatt was hard. A follow-up grope, and he wanted to make out. That wouldn't do. There was sex, and there was moving on, especially when it came to Parker.

Wyatt stripped off his suit jacket and hung it in the closet, followed by his shirt and his trousers. *Fuck*, he was still half-hard, like a horny teenager who didn't get off.

He grazed over his cock, and his need sparked to life at the touch, yanking back vivid images from the afternoon and before. Memories of Parker stroking him through his pants. Of Fiona's faint scent and how it lingered even after she was gone. Of what it felt like, to slide inside her. Watching her writhe in pleasure.

Even of what Parker tasted like.

He stroked in time to the flashes across his senses, harder with each staccato frame. Fiona's gasps. Watching her wrap her lips around Parker's cock. Her mouth crushed against Wyatt's.

He came hard, coating his hand and startling himself with the abrupt intensity. It was a jerk-off. It wasn't supposed to steal his breath.

But maybe now he could get some work done.

He cleaned up, then tugged on some slacks and a polo shirt. Less than five minutes later, his laptop was on the desk, and he was settled in, reading and prioritizing the emails that came in while he was out.

A loud jangling filled the room, and it took him a second ring to register it was his hotel phone. Anyone who wanted to talk to him and knew him would use his cell. Must be the front desk.

He grabbed the receiver. "Yeah."

"Hey, handsome." Devin's voice clawed over him like nails.

Wyatt's first impulse was to hang up, but he needed to know how Devin got his room information. "Afternoon." He kept his tone cool.

"You never called me back." Devin sounded wounded.

"Can't say I ever would have."

"That's fair. Thing is I wanted to talk to you."

Once upon a time, Wyatt fell for the smooth, assured tone. He'd learned. "I assumed that was why you called."

"I missed you."

"No, you didn't." It was difficult to believe

Devin missed anything but fucking with someone's head. Wyatt had sat through the hearing. Saw the things Devin did, both psychologically and physically, to the women he stalked.

"You wound me. Anyway, when you didn't get back to me, I stopped by your office."

Wyatt's stomach dropped into his shoes. This was the second time Devin had done that since being released. He knew things about Wyatt. About their past together. Not the sex—big fucking deal—but the reason Wyatt was compelled to testify against him to begin with. The way Wyatt found out about the stalking. "How'd that go?" he asked.

"They told me you were out of town."

"Hmm… So, how'd you get my hotel info?" Wyatt was tired of beating around the bush.

"Your assistant. Sweet girl. Chatty. Friendly. Tried to assure me you didn't hire her just because of how fuckable she looks in a pencil skirt. But you and I both know it's for the afternoon quickie."

"Sharon excels at her job, which has nothing to do with fucking me."

"Right. Her *job*. So she and I got to chatting, and I mentioned that I know you."

Acid surged up Wyatt's throat.

"Because you were working with me on a sale before your promotion," Devin said.

That was only about half a percent less concerning.

"And she said I could talk to your replacement." Devin sounded conversational, as if he were discussing the weather, rather than giving a detailed description of how he'd gleaned private information about Wyatt's travel plans. "I told her I had some questions for you. She knew what I meant. Once you start working an angle with someone, you want to finish with them. She may have let it drop that you were at the call center.

"Turns out your tastes haven't changed a whole lot, when it comes to lodging. Found you on my second call to business hotels near the offices out there, and it was easy to get someone to patch me up to your room."

Wyatt winced at the run-down. It seemed innocent, but it wasn't. It also sounded disturbingly like the way he'd tracked down Fiona and Parker when they weren't personally open about their whereabouts. *Maybe Devin and I are more alike than I think.* He silenced the nagging voice. "What can I do for you?"

"Have lunch with me when you're back in town. I want to catch up. Talk about that sexy fucking redhead you're seeing. The stripper."

Wyatt's blood turned to ice, and he hung up.

It was a bluff. It had to be. Wyatt had a thing for redheads, and strip clubs were a part of the business, so it was a lucky guess on Devin's part. *Please God, let it be a bluff.* Still, he sent Ginny a quick text along with Devin's name, and told her to be careful.

Then he sent a follow-up, emphasizing she needed to look into him, and please, be extra careful.

If Devin were to talk to the right people at Wyatt's work about the wrong things, what was the worst-case scenario? Mid-level was damage control, after his colleagues found out Wyatt was the one originally charged with felony assault, before he handed over Devin.

But Devin digging into his life? Making his next target personal? Fuck.

♥♥♥

Fiona handed Parker the keys to the rental car as they left the park. One thing she liked about traveling for business, rather than being in a city for his videos, was she could charge the transportation back to the client. They weren't stuck on busses.

She was processing what happened. The entire conversation. It was difficult to think, with Parker running his fingers up the inside of her thigh—an almost absentminded, feather-light touch whenever his hand was free. It wasn't like him, but it was pleasant. Okay, it was enticing and tempting.

They chatted about how her day went, and then his. The parts that came before he ran into Wyatt.

At the hotel, on the elevator ride up, he stood behind her. He teased up the back of her skirt, not pushing it out of the way, but making anticipation thrum over her. She loved it, and it was so out of character for Parker.

Wyatt flipped this switch. She didn't know though—was Parker acting like this out of jealousy or desire or...

Was this what he went through with her?

Parker let them in the room, and before the door finished swinging shut behind them, pinned her to the wall. He slid his hand up between her legs and shoved aside her panties.

She groaned and pressed into him. Her logic forced its way past arousal. "You're as transparent as

I am.”

He kissed along her neck, while he teased his fingers along her slit. He inched closer to her sex, but not enough to offer relief. “I’m trying to see things from a new perspective. Are you complaining?” His words vibrated against her skin.

“No.” She gasped when he sucked on her shoulder. “I want to make sure…”

“Of what?”

“That you’re good with this. With all of it.”

“I don’t know yet. But that kiss… Hearing him talk to you like that again… I’m willing to find out.” He plunged two fingers inside her.

She clenched at the sudden intrusion, then leaned into his touch.

Her phone rang with a familiar tone. “It’s Nick.” She breathed the words.

“Leave it.” Parker pumped at a steady pace. “Unless you’re going to tell him we have a new traveling companion.”

“I’m not.” She reached down to tease her clit while Parker fingered her, and he grabbed her wrist and pinned it to the wall.

Her phone chimed with a new voicemail. Then a text. Then started ringing again.

She sighed and reluctantly extracted herself from the play. “I should see what he wants.” She grabbed her phone and hit *Answer*. “Hey.”

When she looked up at Parker, he made a show of sucking his fingers clean. Slowly. Meticulously. Her pulse hammered in her ears.

“You must have rocked it at the call center,” Nick said. “There’s already an offer on the table.”

"That's awesome." Fiona tried to focus on the conversation and remember she wasn't supposed to have much of an idea this was coming.

"Right? I need a week to run it by Legal, but because we've worked out so many details up front, it won't take much longer. This is ours."

"I'm so excited." Did she sound excited? Did she sound surprised? She needed to. Instead, her mind fluctuated between Parker, the potential for what they could get up to with Wyatt, and wondering if Wyatt had a part in this, despite his assurances. She hated that she couldn't trust him when he said he was hands-off in this process.

"I thought you'd be happier," Nick said. "This is *huge* for us, and you made so much of it possible."

Parker slid up behind her again, and brushed her hair aside to kiss the back of her neck.

"I am. Super excited." She was thrilled about something. Mostly the need between her thighs, and the desire for Parker to finish what he started.

"You almost don't sound surprised." Nick's tone went flat.

Parker glided his hands up her stomach, to tease the bottom of her breasts. She was going to smack him when she was off the phone, but she didn't want him to stop. "We did a good job, and we came in with a reasonable bid." She fought to keep her voice even. I guess I was counting my chickens before they hatched. Probably shouldn't have, but it all worked out."

"You need to stay away from Wyatt."

She pulled the phone away and glared at it. Her brother wasn't reading her mind now, was he? She pulled away from Parker's touch. "Why are you bringing him up?"

"He tried to cost us our company. I don't like him. Why aren't you assuring me it's not an issue?"

Because it was none of Nick's business. "You don't know him."

"You do? This conversation might make me feel better if you said, *Okay, Nick. I get why you're concerned, and I was going to keep my distance anyway.*" Nick's voice held an edge.

So did Fiona's mood. "I shouldn't have to tell you, because it should be a given."

"It *should* be."

She bit the inside of her cheek, to temper her response. Nope. She was losing that struggle. "Maybe I'm reacting to the fact that you think you have a say in my sex life."

Nick sighed. "I'm not… Look—I don't want to fight about that. You know how I feel. I know you're wrong."

"I think you meant that to be funny, but it's not." She spoke through clenched teeth.

"I realized that after I said it. But I swear to God, Fiona, if this man costs us a lucrative deal—"

"Okay. I get why you're concerned. It won't be an issue." She wouldn't promise to stay away from Wyatt, but they'd already agreed on the need for discretion.

Nick's growl crawled up her spine, making her grit her teeth. "Not quite what I was looking for, but close," he said.

"Let me know where I need to be and when, and I'll be there." She was done with this conversation.

How had something so wonderful turned sour?

"Be careful," Nick said.

"I always am."

As she hung up, his doubt sank into her, rather than evaporating. Were she and Parker making the same mistake with Wyatt as last time? Was there an angle she'd missed?

Chapter Nine

Wyatt sat at the back of the conference room, watching Fiona go through her on-boarding presentation, and trying to ignore the occasional glare she sent in his direction.

He didn't expect to get pulled into the meeting, but when the New Orleans office found out he was going to be in town anyway, they said they'd like his input on the implementation.

He didn't protest the opportunity to watch her move and work in couple of hour blocks. And he definitely didn't put up a fight at the suggestion of fifteen-minute one-on-one meetings, to let everyone weigh in on features they'd like to see.

After the morning session of her explanation, Fiona held her individual department-head meetings. Wyatt snagged the first spot, with the excuse that he hadn't expected these meetings. It was tempting to wait until last and take some extra time with her, but the discussions were being held in the fishbowl conference room.

There were times the thought of an audience was tempting. This wasn't one of them.

Fiona gave him a cool smile when he took the seat next to her despite the large conference table.

"You promised me, no more surprises like this," she said before he could offer up any *hello*, witty or otherwise.

He held his hands up. "This is all on the manager in charge. I don't run things this way, and I didn't know about any of this until I got in this morning."

Some of the chill faded from her expression. "That's fair. I only get fifteen minutes with each of you, so we should talk features. What are you looking for?"

"I'm partial to redheads." He couldn't help himself

The way the corner of her mouth tugged up implied she didn't mind. "Is that the only reason you like me?"

"Definitely not." The question caught him off guard, but it shouldn't have. She tended to veer right when he expected a straight line, and that always made him think.

"You also like my pants around my feet?" she asked.

Another hard right, but he was prepared this time. "I'd say the thought keeps me warm at night, but I'm about more than that. Give me some credit."

"Give me a reason to. You're in sales. Sell me on the notion you see more to me."

Nope. Wasn't expecting that at all. "You're not only re-reading *The Siren* for the sex." The answer slipped out easily, propelled by the truth. "It was a gut punch at the end of an intricate story that told you exactly what was coming and yet still surprised you."

"That's where the attraction is to me?"

"That's the tip of the iceberg, because you get the reference and everything behind it." How did she get him to segue from light flirting to an open line to his thoughts? And why didn't he mind? "You yell at movies when they're stupid. You've cut yourself off from living for so long, and now that you've tasted it, you want more. You manage to temper that desire with responsibility. You're sitting across from me, wishing this weren't work, but you'll do your job anyway, despite my best or worst intentions."

Her smile reached her eyes, and she pressed her pen against her bottom lip, to catch the base with her teeth. Such a simple gesture, but it stole the rest of the blood from his brain.

"What brought you back?" he asked. He wasn't going to be the only one exposed in this conversation.

"This is all about the software for me."

He raised his brows. "Insert a joke here about hardware and wetware, and then answer my question. You know I'm not talking about the job. What brought you back?"

She licked her lips. "This."

"Cop-out answer."

"Nope. All-inclusive answer." She leaned in, bringing her several inches closer. Her gaze never left his. "It's because of what you see in the world around you. You look at a person, and you analyze and deconstruct them without breaking a sweat. It's what makes you so good at sales and so shitty at long-term relationships. You overanalyze, and arrogance convinces you the most beneficial answer you is always the right one. And it's not. Not always. When you over-analyze that way, you scare people. You push them away."

He frowned. Opening up was one thing, but he wasn't sure he appreciated her crawling inside his head like… well, the way he tended to do to others. "You're getting to a point, I assume."

"I like it. I love having someone see me for me. You cut right to it, and most people are afraid to do that."

"I have a choice at this point. I can deflect your odd compliment with a joke about wanting to see more of you more often, or I can tell you what I'm actually thinking."

"Let's try that second one. I'd like to see you telling the truth more often."

Ouch. "Phrasing."

"Well-deserved phrasing." She twisted her mouth around the pen, leaving a faint smudge of red on the white plastic.

He envied her pen more than he thought possible. He leaned in as well, until there were only a few inches between them. "All right. The truth. If I thought you'd let me, I'd strip away every layer, a piece at a time—and I'm not talking about clothing—until I saw you. All of you." His voice was low, and her faint scent drifted toward him, tempting and teasing. "And I'd pray to any god who exists that you can do the same for me."

"I'd like to." Her reply was breathy.

He straightened, needing the distance to clear

his head and remind himself they were on display. "Your next appointment is in five."

"Yeah." She nodded and shuffled the stack of papers in front of her. Pink dotted her cheeks.

"As for software features, tell me what it does and what everyone else is asking for, and I'll sell it."

She stood, and he did the same. "It was a pleasure meeting with you, Mr. Lindberg." She shook his hand, and the need inside ran faster.

"I'm hoping for more one-on-one sessions." He slid back toward casual and playful. "If you've time later, they've set me up with a temporary office. I'd love to chat in more detail about my requirements for what you're offering."

She stepped back, expression neutral. The only hint of what she was thinking was the pink racing down her neck and over her chest, which heaved with each breath. "I'll see if I can break away this afternoon."

♥♥♥

Wyatt looked up at a knock on his office door, and couldn't hide his grin when he saw Fiona.

"Do you have a little time to talk?" Her voice wavered on the last word.

God, yes. "Come on in." He stood and closed the door behind her. When he pushed the lock in place, a smile whispered across her face, and he was instantly hard.

"I was hoping to explore next steps, based on our conversation this morning."

The professional, vague lead-in was a turn-on too. Or perhaps it was because she was the one saying it. He should be more worried about how easy it was to let his guard down when she was around.

"I was hoping the same." He stepped closer, until his body pressed against hers, then nudged her back toward the desk. "Before we get started, are there any restrictions I should be aware of?"

"Don't leave any visible marks." She licked her bottom lip.

He knotted his fingers in her hair and yanked her head back. Her gasp was a direct line to his erection. He bit her earlobe, growling against her skin. "*Fuck*, I missed you." He moved his hands to her hips and lifted her to sit on the desk.

"I hope so." Her tone was playful.

Not the answer he expected. "You do?"

"You went to a lot of trouble, to get us to this point." She tilted her head up and met his gaze, her lips close enough to his that he felt her breath. "I hope I'm worth it."

He wanted to kiss her. Taste the shine of red. He also liked the anticipation. "So far. Are you complaining?"

"I should be, all things considered. I should be over you. Should have moved on. Not let you haunt my dreams. And— Don't you have a way to shut me up?"

He crushed his mouth to hers, sinking into the sensation and into her moan. The buildup was nice, but now that he had her, his restraint was gone. He glided his hand down the front of her blouse, undid the first few buttons, and tugged the fabric open.

Wyatt kissed along her jaw and then down her chest, to suck and bite the tantalizing swell of her breast above her bra. "No visible marks. I can do that," he murmured against her skin.

He scraped his fingers up her legs, pushing her skirt out of the way, and slid between her thighs. She traced his cock through his trousers, drawing his nerves to life. *No marks above the collar.* He tried to keep the request at the front of his mind, as he wove his fingers in her hair and yanked her head back.

Fiona's whimper-squeal was better than smooth whiskey searing through his veins.

He kissed her neck, then lower. "*Fuck*, I missed you. The sounds you make. The way you smell. Your sexy brain." He teased his finger over the leg of her panties and underneath the crotch. Her juices coated his skin. "Fucking your tight, wet cunt."

"You say the sweetest things." She dragged down his zipper.

Her cool touch on his warm shaft made him groan. He'd love to draw this out, but part of the fun was that they were running on borrowed time, and he didn't know how much. Fortunately, he had the presence of mind to roll on a condom before the impulse to drive inside her wiped away his reason.

He gripped her hips tight and nudged her opening with the head of his dick. "I mean every word."

When he plunged inside Fiona, her mischievous smile melted into a silent gasp. Her pussy hugged him and drew him in. Restraint vanished, and he slammed into her hard and fast. "Play with yourself," he whispered against her cheek.

She slid her hand between them, and her fingers brushed his cock with each thrust. "I wish we had more time."

"Tell me what you'd want if we weren't on the clock." The conversation was the right level of distracting. Without it, Wyatt wouldn't be able to hold back.

Her breath came in short gasps, and she thrust against him to the pace he set. "You'd have to surprise me." Her words were punctuated. "I'd be blindfolded and tied up."

"I like the way you think." His head swam, as the fresh images mingled with the feelings of here and now.

"But I hope at some point it involves sucking you off while Parker fucks me." Her voice hitched on *Parker*, and she met his gaze.

He should be bothered she brought Parker into the fantasy, but he liked it. "With him stroking your clit, the way you're doing now?"

"God, yes." Her gasps came in staccato bursts, and when she came, she bit her lip hard enough he saw the pale impressions around her teeth. She squeezed him tight, clenching and spasming.

Before she could pull her hand away, he covered it with his own. "Keep fingering yourself." The command came out as a grunt.

She nodded and slid into another orgasm, milking him.

Desire tightened in his balls, and flashes danced behind his eyelids. He buried his head against her breast, biting when he came, to keep silent.

As he stopped, a lightheaded sensation sank in, and his knees threatened to stop supporting him.

He dug his knuckles into the desk, to hold

himself up, and rested his forehead against the crook of her neck.

For a moment, the only sound in the room was their heavy breathing. He hadn't gotten off like that in… He didn't know how long it had been. Even the last time he was with her, it wasn't so potent.

What was it about this woman that unraveled him?

"I'm going to say something I probably shouldn't." Fiona's breath was hot on his cheek.

He clenched his jaw, grateful she couldn't see. "What?"

"When you say you're sorry for what happened, I'm desperate for you to mean it."

It hurt that she didn't believe him, but he didn't blame her. "I only know one way to prove it, and that's to show you."

She sighed and leaned her head against his. "Sometimes I think I'm stupid, trusting you a second time after what you did. I keep telling myself this is me giving you the rope to hang yourself with, but… don't fuck me over."

The sharp edge lining her pleading gnawed at him.

A rumble rolled through the room, shaking the floor and rattling the windows.

Fiona frowned. "What was that?"

The blare of the fire alarms drowned out the end of her question. Wyatt's phone beeped, and Reception's voice came over the line. "This is not a drill. Everyone please evacuate the building immediately." The woman's voice quivered.

The hammering in Wyatt's ears was no longer

from exertion. What was going on? The faint smell of smoke drifted into the room, mingling with Fiona's scent and that of sex.

Wyatt stepped back, discarded his condom, and zipped up, while Fiona stood and straightened her clothes.

"How do I look?" Her question was hurried.

He didn't know what this was, but urgency sped through his veins. "Like you didn't just get pinned to a desk and fucked."

"Good."

They stepped into the hallway and the rush of people heading for exits. No one knew what had happened, but tension crackled through the air.

Wyatt had a sinkingly bad feeling about this.

Chapter Ten

Parker sat at the bar in a local microbrewery. A baseball game played on the TV on the wall, and he watched without registering what was going on.

He should be filming today. Or scouting places to film. Or editing. Something. Fiona's offhanded comments from the other day—her observation that his voice had changed on camera—rolled in his head.

Then there were Wyatt's words, that Parker wouldn't be happy with the status quo of a regular relationship. The bastard shouldn't be under Parker's skin, but he was.

Why wasn't he more jealous about this agreement with Wyatt? Instead, each time he came back it, expecting envy over having to share Fiona, anticipation flooded him.

Seeing the world, filming and sharing the experiences with his audience, was supposed to be fun. For a long time, it had been. For the last couple of months, it felt like he'd lost sight of all of that. Too many rules. Too many guidelines. Not enough freedom.

Was bringing Wyatt into their relationship a defiance of that, or the first step toward fixing things?

Logic that sounded a lot like Nick warred with Parker's instinct.

"Who's winning?" A male voice jarred him from questions with no answers.

Parker looked to his side, to see who sat next to him. The man was probably a few years older— closer to Wyatt's age—striking, with a scruff of light beard and mussed blond hair.

"I'm sorry—what?" Parker asked.

Mr. Handsome nodded at the TV. "Who's winning?"

"Uh… The home team?"

The guy chuckled. "I'm not much of a fan, so I wouldn't know the difference, but the way you were staring at it, I figured you must be into the game."

"It was in my line of sight." Parker was grateful for the excuse to climb out of his own head.

"I know how that works. Mind if I join your staring off into space?"

"I think I'm done with that for now."

"Devin." The man extended his hand.

Parker shook it. "Parker."

"I know." Devin ducked his head. "Not to be all creepy stalker—I'm a fan of your show."

"Oh yeah?" Words Parker liked hearing on most days, but were an extra boost right now.

"I saw you over here, alone, and I had to find out if you were as friendly in person."

"What's the verdict?"

"Too soon to tell." Devin grinned.

Parker couldn't have asked for better, more low-key company. There was no expectation here. No burning questions raised. "It's always nice to meet a fan. Join me for a drink?"

"Only if it's Coke. I'm on my lunch break." Devin had a plate of fries and a bowl of soup in front of him.

Parker must have *really* been in another place, to not have seen him sit and be served. "At ten thirty in the morning?"

"Says the man knocking back a bottle of amber ale. And technically, it's almost eleven. I work at the shipping building, so I start early. Lunch early."

Get off early. Parker expected the words and was relieved not to hear them. Not that he'd mind this guy hitting on him, but it was nice to have a conversation that wasn't raw aggression with the guy trying to fuck his girlfriend.

Speaking of Wyatt… It was a bit of a coincidence Devin worked at the same place. But in a town this size, a decent percentage of people probably did.

Parker was curious, though. "Do you know Wyatt Lindberg?"

Devin covered his mouth and dropped his gaze. "Of course. That is… not personally, but everyone knows him. He's the Senior Vice President of Sales and Marketing. Have you worked with him?"

Parker shook his head. He wasn't going to give away too much info, especially if it led back to Fiona. "I had a friend who pitched him something. A vendor."

"Did you meet him?"

Parker gave a noncommittal shrug. "Why?"

"I've always wondered if he was as much larger than life in person as he seems."

Was Devin blushing? Did everyone have a crush on Wyatt? Okay, so Parker might be exaggerating a little. "He's a salesman and the boss. I assume he has presence."

"Right? He's so sexy. Sorry. That's probably inappropriate."

So much for getting Wyatt off Parker's mind. "It's okay. Everyone's got a type."

"What's yours?" Devin asked.

"I'm versatile." It might be time to wrap this up. Parker looked around, thinking of a polite way to make his exit. His gaze fell on the TV.

The game was gone, replaced with a *Breaking News* banner. The shipping building was on the screen, next to the anchor. Smoke billowed from the unit the camera was focused on.

Parker grabbed the remote from the counter and turned up the sound.

"…an explosion rocked the shipping center this morning—"

"*Christ.*" Devin pushed back so quickly, his stool scraped against the tile. "I need to check in. Make sure my co-workers are all right."

"Yeah." Parker knew the feeling. The gnawing in his gut wouldn't go away. He dialed Fiona. At the same time he scanned the evacuated crowds on the TV, searching for her face.

Fiona stood several feet back from anyone else.

Her primary contact was exchanging information with colleagues, though no one really knew what was going on. The ripple of rumor running through the pockets of people outside was that a package had exploded, and the bomb squad was currently checking to make sure it was the only one.

Two people had mild injuries, but no one else had been hurt, that she'd heard. The entire thing made her ill. Why would someone mail a bomb?

She hugged herself. What should she be doing? She'd rather be talking to Wyatt, but for appearances' sake that seemed like a bad idea. Besides, he was on the phone with his home office, exchanging information like everyone else.

Her phone rang, and she reached for it, grateful for the distraction. When she saw Parker's name and face on the screen, guilt whispered inside. "Hey," she answered.

"Red. I saw the building on the news. Are you all right?" Panic filled his question.

She should have called him right away, instead of milling around like a lost kitten. "I'm fine. We weren't anywhere near the explosion."

"Thank God."

His concern warmed her, and cemented in her mind how lucky she was to have him in her life. "We're not going to get any more work done today," she said. "As soon as the police give us the *all clear*, one way or the other, I'll head back to the hotel."

"Good. Stay safe, and I love you."

"I love you too." She disconnected. Such simple words, and every time he said them, a warm glow spread through her.

Fiona lost track of how long she waited before everyone was allowed to either go back to work or home. Her stomach was growling, and she'd run out of free lives on every game she could access from her phone.

She sent Wyatt a, *Thanks for your time.* No reason to give him something he had to explain if anyone was looking over his shoulder. He glanced in her direction and gave her the briefest of smiles, before turning back to the person he was talking to.

Parker greeted Fiona seconds after she walked into their room. He cupped her face in his hands and pressed a hard kiss to her mouth. She gasped against his lips.

"I'm glad you're all right," he said when he broke away. "Is everyone else okay?"

"You know as much as me, from what I read on the news sites. No serious injuries."

"Good. Come lose the work clothes." He grasped her fingers and tugged her into the bedroom.

She stepped out of her shoes and left them by the door. As Parker trailed his fingers down the front of her blouse, similarly to what Wyatt had done just a few hours ago, the guilt returned. She should have thought about it sooner, but she let herself get wrapped up in the moment.

Just because she and Parker agreed to experiment with Wyatt, didn't mean it was okay for her to do it alone.

Parker tugged the sides of her blouse aside. A frown ghosted over his face, and he brushed a touch across the fresh bite mark on her breast. "That's new."

"I'm—" She covered his hand with hers. She was what? Sorry? Not that it happened. But she would be, if it upset him. "Are you mad?"

He drew tiny circles along her skin with his thumb, rather than pulling away. "I should be. I pictured this as being both of us. Especially at first."

"I should have thought about—"

He kissed her lightly, but it was enough to silence the thought. "It's okay."

"It is?" Why was she questioning him?

He nodded. "I didn't realize it until I saw this." He brushed his lips over the bite mark. "I need to either be all right with what you're doing or not. I can't keep fluctuating. And I landed on *I am*. I keep thinking about the argument with Nick and how much his view bothered me. How much I don't agree with what he said. I should take issue by this thing with Wyatt. But the longer I think about it, the more I'm good with things. Let's have fun with it."

"You were part of the fantasy." She wasn't certainif she should mention that or not, but she'd rather be open about everything.

His smirk was worth the confession. "How'd that go?"

"Well enough that I hope you're part of the reality next time. I have a favor to ask, though, despite having used up so many by now. If you hook up with him or anyone else, without me there, I want details." As she made the request, desire flowed through her. It was a different type of voyeurism, and it was delicious.

Parker cupped her breast and squeezed, pinching her nipple through the lace of her bra. "I'll agree to that," he said. "For now, will you settle for something ordinary, like a shower? I'll help get you clean."

"Somehow I doubt the second part, but okay."

Fiona grabbed her phone when it rang, and frowned at the unfamiliar number. "Hello?"

"May I speak with Fiona Walters?" The man's tone was cool and professional.

Her gut twisted at the unfamiliar voice. It was nothing. She used this line for work, so it was probably someone from the shipping company. "This is she."

"This is Detective Marshall. We're talking to several people who were at the shipping company today, and I'm wondering if you could come down and answer some questions for us."

"Oh." What was she supposed to say? *No?*

"You're not a suspect. These are routine investigation questions." His tone softened.

"Of course. I understand. I can be there in about half an hour. Should I ask for anyone?"

This was real life, not a TV show made to be all suspense and no reality, so when he said this was routine, there was nothing for her to worry about. Right?

Chapter Eleven

Fiona sat across from Detective Marshall in an exam room. He warned her that, even though she wasn't a suspect, if she became one at any point, anything she said today would be on record.

She didn't like the sound of that.

"I'm not saying I think you will be. I'm simply required to warn you of that fact." His voice was kind.

She was only mildly reassured. "This whole thing is horrible, so whatever I can do to help…"

He slid a flat, sealed plastic bag across the table. "This is what we found near the explosion site."

It was one of her business cards. Seeing the same design she looked at every day, but half-burned, made her stomach churn. "What do you need to know about it?"

"Is that your handwriting on the back?"

She flipped it over, and the sickness building inside surged in her throat. It said *Parker,* next to his phone number. "No." She recognized the block of the *a*, though, and the hook on the *2*s.

"Do you know whose handwriting it is?" Detective Marshall asked.

She had to be wrong. Remembering incorrectly, because Wyatt always hovered at the back of her mind and this was a stressful situation. There was no way the handwriting matched the business card he'd given her—the one she still had in the front pocket of her carry-on bag.

"I don't. I'm sorry," she said.

"It's all right." He pushed a notepad toward her. "I'm sorry to ask this, but I need you to rewrite what's on the card, three times."

"It's my boyfriend's name and phone number. I wouldn't put that on information I gave to a client." She did as he asked anyway, and handed the notepad back. Her handwriting didn't look anything like that on the card.

"Can you tell me who you've given these to, recently?"

She tried to keep a barking laugh from slipping out. "I'm traveling for business, and before this, I was involved in pitching our product to this company. I expect I've given out fifty or more of these to their people in the past couple of weeks."

"Did any of them strike you as... off?"

She scowled. "Could you be any more vague?" She wanted to be helpful but had no idea what he was fishing for.

"Someone saw fit to write your boyfriend's information on your business card. I'm wondering if you have any idea why."

Fiona scrubbed her face, sighing through her

fingers. "He doesn't have anything to do with my work, and I don't introduce him to most of my clients." Except Wyatt. "I was stalked a short while ago, and he was there for large parts of that."

"I did pull up the records about that incident." Detective Marshall's kind tone was back, and the corners of his eyes softened. "Can you tell me in your own words what happened?"

She really didn't want to. The dreams were mostly gone, and she was grateful to leave the incident with Tim in the past. "Is it relevant?"

"Probably not. But we're looking for a bombing suspect and have to examine everything. We're talking to every person who shipped or was receiving a package that was supposed to be on that truck, and we're talking to you because of this." He tapped the card.

"Right." She took a deep breath and launched into the story.

With each new nudge for details, she was left feeling rawer and more exposed. He never asked why she hadn't paid attention to the signs, but she wondered how she could have been so stupid to let something like that happen.

By the time the interview ended, she'd been turned inside-out, stomped on, and shoved back into her skin.

She stood when the detective did, and shook his hand.

"I'll be in touch if we need anything else, but I think we're done. Thank you for your time," he said.

She walked to the lobby, numb and feeling like an exposed nerve in one bundle. Parker stood the moment she stepped through the door, and met her, hug her.

She rested her forehead against his chest, wanting to sink into the embrace.

"Should I ask how it went?" His lips moved against the top of her head.

"No. Not here." She fisted his shirt, needing the foundation to hold onto, to keep from slipping away.

He held her until her grip relaxed, then guided her toward the parking garage. "Let's get out of here."

"Okay." The sooner they got back to the hotel, the better, so she could fall apart in the pit of reliving what happened with Tim.

Parker drove back to the hotel, not talking and with the radio off. She was as grateful for the silence as she was for the way he let her squeeze his hand tight when he didn't need it to navigate.

They made it back to their room, and she sank onto the couch. Parker sat next to her and pulled her close. "What can I do?"

"He asked me about Tim. I'll be okay, but I need it out of my head." The words came out with more desperation than she intended.

"What will do that?"

Not horror. No action—too many explosions. And a romantic comedy could be sweet, but it could be one of those with all the wrong triggers. "I don't know."

"I've got the perfect thing. Wait here." He returned a moment later with his laptop, set it on the coffee table, and pulled up *Bill and Ted's Excellent Adventure.*

He and rubbed her back gently as the movie started.

Between the two of them, they knew ninety-nine percent of the lines. Sometimes they talked in unison, and at others they took turns.

It helped bring Fiona back to a neutral place, and drove memories of the stalking to the back of her mind.

The film ended and faded into the next, and she and Parker drifted off on the couch.

She woke up to a dark laptop screen and Parker sleeping soundly.

It wasn't only the awkward position on the sofa that had woken her, though. It was a dream. She grasped for strands of it, but they were out of her reach.

Given how her day went, she'd consider herself grateful.

She shook Parker gently, until he woke up. "We should go to bed," she said.

"Right. Bed." He stood with her and stretched his neck. "Be right there."

He wandered into the bathroom, and she made her way to the bedroom.

She sat on the mattress, and her carry-on bag caught her attention. She dug for the familiar business card in the front pocket, not sure why it seemed so important she look at it now.

Wyatt's name and number stared back at her, scrawled in the same handwriting she'd seen on the back of her card at the police station.

It was a coincidence. She was one of hundreds they would interview, and he worked for the company.

"Everything all right?" Parker's question startled her.

She shoved Wyatt's business card back in her bag. "Fine. I'm tired. Spacing off."

"It was a long day. Come on. Clothes off. Let's sleep."

"Right." A long day, a bunch of circumstantial evidence, and the detective told her the card probably had nothing to do with the bombing. She'd call the station in the morning, let him know it might be Wyatt's card, and it wouldn't be a big deal.

None of the logic or self-assurance got rid of the clawing sensation inside.

Chapter Twelve

Wyatt wouldn't pace the sidewalk next to the bar.

He'd spent the last couple of days cooped up in a hotel room, working, because office space was limited after the bombing. His morning quickie with Fiona had done the opposite of clearing her out of his thoughts, and he'd had to answer some odd questions from the police about one of her business cards.

However, he refused to let the excess energy coursing through him show. This was a new city with new possibilities, and a full Saturday night stretched in front of him.

He wouldn't give a second thought to the fact that Parker insisted on meeting him near their first destination, rather than giving Wyatt a room number. They were all staying in the same hotel, because his company had a contract with this chain, and it was implied the evening would lead to sex. But sure—no reason to trust him with which room they were staying in.

He didn't know if it was more or less ridiculous, given the meeting spot was within walking distance of where they were all staying. A lot of the places Wyatt knew about were; he'd rather take a stroll from his hotel room to find a local place for the evening, than spend time driving around for something that might or might not pan out.

"We're not late, are we?" Fiona's comment drew a smile and softened the edges of his mood.

He turned to see them approaching from the opposite direction of the hotel. "No. I'm early. Couldn't sit still in my room anymore and needed some air."

Parker looked him over. That gaze traveling along Wyatt's body sent need racing through him. "You lose your luggage?" Parker's tone was light.

Wyatt chuckled. "No. This is more appropriate to the setting."

"You own a Def Leopard T-shirt. And you're wearing it in public." Fiona traced her fingers over the faded screen print.

Wyatt sucked in a sharp breath at the feather-light touch. "I can take it off if you want."

She bit her bottom lip. "Maybe."

"You should have called," Parker said. "We were checking out this antiques place a viewer recommended, and... Let's just say it was droppable."

People jostled around them, some heading to the bar Wyatt picked out, and others scurrying off in the summer night for other distractions.

"Not a fan of classic electronics?" Wyatt let a hint of teasing slide into his voice. He could guess where they'd been. There was a shop a few blocks away that specialized in mid-twentieth-century appliances. It was kind of neat to walk by, but it picked up new ownership a few years back and had become more of a junk shop.

Parker shrugged. "The girl behind the counter was nice enough to let me film, but it was kind of sad. Everything in there was broken."

"Broken things need love too," Fiona's said softly. "Speaking of… Do you have that business card I gave you?"

The first comment hung heavy, despite her attempt to gloss over it. She didn't see herself as broken, did she? He'd focus more on the thought if her question didn't remind him of the other reason he was feeling the lack of trust. "Not on me. Why?"

"Did you write Parker's name on it?" she asked. Any emotion had vanished from her voice.

Wyatt might be jumping to conclusions, but it seemed fair to guess she was asking because she knew about the card the police questioned him about. "Don't know why I would. He called me, so his number's in my phone. Why?" he asked again.

She shrugged. "Me being weird."

"All right." Wyatt could push the issue, but he'd already brushed off the conversation with the police and wanted to enjoy the night. "Since the antique shop was a bust, I've got something a little more camera friendly if you want."

From the outside, the place was another windowless building in the middle of a strip of shops, defying his promise of an interesting evening. He knew what was inside, though, and wasn't concerned.

Fiona glanced at the sign on the shop front, then looked again. "The Dungeon? If you run into anyone from work, it's going to be hard to justify the whole notion of *showing a vendor a good time* and keep it innocent."

"You filthy girl."

"Like you're complaining," Parker said.

"Not in the least, but it's not that kind of dungeon. It also doesn't have dragons."

Fiona's pout was exaggerated. "You're taking all the fun out of this."

This was much better than dancing around how much they did or didn't trust him. "Give it a chance," Wyatt said.

"I found this place online, but Google said it was closed permanently." Parker pulled a handheld camera from his bag.

"Yeah. They don't know why that is. They keep trying to get it fixed, but nope." Wyatt held open the door. "The locals know better, though. And I talked to the owner. They typically have a strict no-camera policy, but he's willing to make an exception for you."

Parker studied him, brow furrowed. "Why?"

"Because he likes me. And I talked up your channel, so he likes you, too."

"Smart man." Fiona brushed past them both and stepped into the corridor. "Though I'm still not impressed."

"Keep walking." Wyatt nudged her forward, and Parker joined them.

The hallway was dimly lit, with concrete walls

and floor. Wyatt had never seen it in full light and wasn't interested in doing so. This was part of the experience.

They turned a corner, and then another, and stepped into a massive courtyard. The roof was one big skylight, letting in a view of the night. Wrought iron tables sat on the concrete patio. The bar was to the right, hiding the kitchen from view, and there was a stage at the far end of the clearing.

"Wow." Fiona's gaze fell on the centerpiece of the bar.

Parker trained his camera on the iron dragon sculpture that guarded the stage. Its wings spanned the length of the raised platform, and its head was pointed toward the sky, as if it were about to take flight.

"Okay. So there's one dragon," Wyatt said.

A hostess showed them to a table, as Parker and Fiona continued to look around. "There are manacles on the wall, and bars." She pointed, and he followed with the camera.

Fiona turned back to Wyatt. "You don't look impressed."

"I've seen it before." He thought the place was kind of neat, but seeing it through their eyes... He'd forgotten what a difference the first time experience was.

"I would make a stop here every time I had a connecting flight, to remember how epic that beast is." Parker nodded at the sculpture.

Wyatt mostly came here because they had good beer and music. The heavy metal wasn't always his thing, but when he was in the right mood, screaming guitars and voices were good company.

They chatted about some of the history of the place and gave their orders to the waiter.

"Hey." Wyatt stopped him before he could walk away. "Who's playing tonight?"

"Open mic. The house band is backing up anyone willing to risk their skin up there." It was hard to tell from his voice if the idea amused him or left him disgusted.

When he was gone, Fiona grabbed Parker's hand. "You should take a turn."

"Nope. Definitely not. I'm filming." Parker shook the camera, emphasizing his point.

"You sing, too." Wyatt was hesitantly impressed.

"In the car. In the shower. Same places as most people." Parker almost looked embarrassed. Almost.

It was cute.

The thought caught Wyatt off-guard. "I'll take your word for it. I didn't plan anything else for tonight. I wasn't sure how long we'd want to stay, and I figured we'd wrap up the evening in my room. But I have a couple of things to pick from tomorrow, depending on what you're in the mood for."

"Like what?" Fiona leaned in, her attention on him.

As he ran through the list, the band started warm-ups. The waiter returned with their food— Wyatt promised, if they got the appetizer sampler, they could try a little bit of everything and be satisfied without being overwhelmed.

The band warmed up, playing a series of generic riffs and chords set to a simple drum beat.

Wyatt, Parker, and Fiona chatted some more while they ate.

"Ladies and gentlemen, welcome to open night mic at The Dungeon." A booming voice carried from the stage. Gabe was in his late forties. His hair was silver around the temples, but that was the only obvious hint of his age. He filled out the black T-shirt with a defined chest and stomach, as though the clothes were painted on. Tattoos snaked up his arms and vanished under his sleeves, to reappear above his collar.

Wyatt nodded at the guy behind the mic. "That's Gabe. The owner. I'll introduce you in a little bit if you'd like. He was in L.A. in the eighties and managed a couple of midrange garage bands."

"Cool." Parker looked impressed. He turned his camera to Gabe.

"Up tonight, we have a local favorite," Gabe said. A murmur ran through the crowd. That was strange. "He loves you at least as much as you love him. Let's give a loud round of applause to Bill."

There was a smattering of claps, but most people kept their attention on their own plates.

"Tough crowd," Fiona said.

Wyatt had to agree. He was about to turn back to their plans for tomorrow, when the band kicked up, louder than before.

The opening chords were for "Africa" by Toto. Bill sang, and Wyatt winced.

Parker cringed and set down his camera.

"What he lacks in tone, he makes up for in enthusiasm." Fiona scrunched her face when Bill hit another flat note, a full beat before the band reached that part of the song.

"*So,*" Wyatt raised his voice to be heard, and partly to help himself ignore the signing. "Peace Gardens and lunch tomorrow?"

They fell back into the conversation, all three of them groaning when Bill did another song. When he started on his third, Wyatt excused himself. "I'll be right back."

He sought out Gabe and hoped Parker would forgive him for what he was about to do. Wyatt returned to the table a moment later. Gabe stepped on stage as the last strains of Bills song faded away.

"Thank you for that. Can we get a round of applause for Bill?" Gabe said.

The clapping was much louder this time, and Bill grinned and reached for the mic.

Gabe stepped out of his reach. "We've got a new singer on the docket, and he's going to make us famous. Let's give it up for Parker."

"No." Parker glared at Wyatt. "I do behind the camera."

"Bullshit. You spend half your time talking directly into the thing." Wyatt turned to Fiona. "Is he good?"

"He's incredible. Cross my heart." Fiona didn't hesitate. She stood and tugged Parker to his feet.

Parker shook his head but walked toward the stage, amid growing cheers. He exchanged a few words with Gabe and the band, away from the mic.

Wyatt grabbed the camera, and Fiona glared. "What are you doing?"

"Footage. His fans will eat this up."

She twisted her mouth, but relaxed. "It's true."

The opening strains of "Eyes of a Stranger" by Queensrÿche played.

"He's not old enough to know this," Wyatt said.

Fiona rolled her eyes. "And you are? I swear to you, he can hit those notes in a way Jeff Tate lost long ago."

Wyatt hoped so. The crowd was kind enough to Bill, but he didn't know if they'd be happy having one eye-watering act replace the other.

When Parker started to sing, Wyatt's jaw dropped, and he snapped his mouth shut again. Parker wasn't blow-away-the-judges-on-The-Voice incredible—Fiona was a little biased—but he was good, and he was a welcome change.

It was a haunting song, and when Parker hit the chorus and the high notes, Wyatt swallowed past a lump. There was a hint of pain there that made the music come alive.

He glanced at Fiona, who watched the performance with the sweetest look of adoration. A fist clenched around his chest. He ignored it and kept filming.

When Parker finished to deafening cheers, Gabe had someone else waiting to take the stage. Parker strode back to their table. He cast an eyebrow-raised look at Wyatt, then bent at the waist to give Fiona a long kiss.

Watching the exchange through the lens filled Wyatt with a strange cocktail of being removed and being too close to such an intimate moment. He pressed *Stop* and set the camera on the table. "You need to post this."

"Yeah, yeah. I'll clean it up tomorrow. Thank

you for filming," Parker said.

"You two have anything that doesn't make the site?" Wyatt liked the thought. "Of the explicit, naked, fucking variety?"

Fiona blushed. *God*, he loved that look, especially the way the pink spread down her long neck.

Parker's jaw tightened, but he relaxed it so quickly, it might have been nothing. "If it *did* exist—and I'm not saying it does—I'd rather no one knew. I'd hate for something like that to get out."

Wyatt didn't care for the tone. "If I asked roughly, could I get a private copy?"

"No." Fiona replied too quickly for his liking.

Of course. Because they didn't trust him. A truth that burned far more than he wanted to admit.

Chapter Thirteen

Parker didn't want tonight to fall apart. Being on stage, being *here*, sent a thrill running through him and reminded him why he enjoyed this entire video-journal thing. It added to the low thrum of anticipation that had been humming in his veins all day.

There were points he wouldn't yield on, for the sake of Wyatt's ego, but there were alternatives as well.

"You're welcome to a hands-on demonstration of the real thing, instead of video," Parker offered.

Fiona's mischievous smile defied the shy duck of her head. "I like the sound of that."

Wyatt's expression relaxed. "Is that your way of suggesting we get out of here?"

"I don't know." Parker struggled to keep a straight face. "If we stick around, Bill might do another set."

"Or we could push you back on stage." Wyatt held his gaze, unflinching.

Parker didn't have an issue with performing, and singing had been a nice buzz, but he wasn't in the mood for that now. The shift in conversation reminded him of what the goal at the end of the night. It also filled his head with snippets of the video he did have of Fiona, lying naked on a hotel bed, writing in pleasure while she gave him a private show.

He shook his head, partly to refuse Wyatt, but mostly to rattle the vivid images aside.

"Leaving sounds good," Fiona said.

All three of them reached for their wallets at the same time.

"Let me. Vendor dinner, remember?" Wyatt's tone left no room for argument.

Conflict nudged Parker's thoughts, wavering between relief that someone else picked up the tab, and hating that whipping out that black card came so easily for Wyatt. He stowed the feeling. When the bill was paid, he stood and offered Fiona a hand, to tug her to her feet.

"Do you want the mini-tour between here and the hotel?" Wyatt asked.

"Sure." Parker enjoyed Wyatt's tours. Wyatt knew these places and talked about them in a way that breathed a different light into each city.

Parker kept his camera out, recording as they strolled down the sidewalk. Wyatt pointed out different historical spots, but he also had mildly personal stories to tell. Where he was when he met the starting line-up for the Chicago Bulls during the playoffs. Why he was in town when he helped a local celebrity change a tire.

It was fun and interesting and so much better

than the dreck Parker had been feeding into his videos for the last couple of weeks. This had a flavor beyond *looked it up on Google*.

The storytelling was punctuated with the occasional giggle or gasp from Fiona. Out of the corner of his eye, Parker saw Wyatt glide a hand up her legs and under her skirt.

She bit her bottom lip, rather than pulling away.

"You're not wearing anything under your dress." Wyatt's tone held a blend of scolding and desire.

Fiona smirked. "Nope."

Wyatt glanced at Parker. "Too bad none of this goes on camera."

"I've got my memories." Parker laughed the comment off, but it lingered. Wyatt was right; Parker missed the carefree side of this. But he wanted it with Fiona, and he was tired of playing by the competition rules.

It was a means to an end, though.

Fuck it. Like the other footage he had, just because this existed didn't mean anyone else had to see it. He spun the camera toward Fiona and Wyatt. "What am I missing?"

"Nothing." Fiona swatted Wyatt's hand away.

Wyatt twisted and grabbed her wrist, eliciting a surprised squeak. He raised her fingers to his mouth and sucked on one, lavishing attention on it. Fiona's lips parted, and her eyelids fluttered half-closed, a quiet sigh escaping when Wyatt let her go.

"Absolutely nothing," Wyatt agreed.

The most teasing, sensual sort of *nothing*.

Parker's erection strained against his jeans. It

was different, watching it through the viewfinder of a camera. "You've got me torn. I don't know if I'd rather capture this or be a part of it."

They were walking at a snail's pace now, and the few other pedestrians brushed past them in irritation. Parker didn't care. He was focused on more important things.

Fiona's smile was mischievous. "There's an easy solution."

"There is?" Besides getting back to the hotel as quickly as possible and setting up his tripod? Because he didn't have the patience for that.

She nodded. "I'll capture it, and *you* participate." She stepped close to press her frame against his, her hip digging into his cock. Her breath was hot on his skin. She snagged his camera and twirled away. "Now you can join in."

Parker opened his mouth to argue, but Wyatt kissed him before he could speak. It was a hard, hungry crush of mouths. Fiona's delighted giggle matched Parker's groan, and—*fuck*—how did this feel so good?

Wyatt pulled back to meet his gaze, and the air between them threatened to ignite. "Are you thinking what I'm thinking?" Wyatt asked.

Parker wasn't sure. "That if we keep doing this on the street, things will get indecent real fast?"

"Eh... I was thinking I want a copy of everything that's recorded tonight. But clothes coming off is involved, so I'd say we're on the same page."

"Parker has work to do. Videos to produce." Fiona's tone was difficult to read.

Wyatt shrugged. "So let's finish this tour. I'll keep narrating."

It was going to be near impossible to think, since all the blood had rushed from Parker's head, but he could point the lens at things. Fiona handed his camera back, and they resumed their stroll.

"That restaurant over there doesn't look like much on the outside, but it's nice inside. Four stars, easily." Wyatt gestured at a brick-faced building on the other side of the street. "Crystal wine glasses, cotton tablecloths—the works."

"Classy." Fiona sounded impressed.

"Perfect for feeling someone up underneath."

Parker rolled his eyes, but he was smiling. He wasn't going to be able to use any of the sound from these clips, and he was fine with that. "You know from experience?"

"Nah." Wyatt shook his head. "But I've always wanted to find out, if you're volunteering."

"Pout," Fiona said.

"What's wrong?" Parker suspected it was nothing serious, from the way her lips were quirked up.

She forced her lower lip out. "I'm not sure if I'd rather be the volunteer, or watch the two of you."

"*Fuck*, I love the way your mind works." Wyatt's voice was gravelly.

Parker agreed with both of their statements. The rest of the walk was filled with Wyatt's wish list of places he figured were good for getting off. The trip was both too long and over too soon.

They stepped onto the elevator together. "Keep recording," Wyatt said as he pressed the button for his floor.

Parker did, watching both real life and the tiny screen in front of him, as Wyatt teased his hand under Fiona's skirt again, making her squirm.

The few seconds it took to reach their destination left Parker so hard it ached. It was an odd sensation. A step between participant and voyeur, intimate and public at the same time.

They reached Wyatt's room. Parker hung back to capture the scene. It was like watching a film, but still being so close he could reach out and touch.

"Stay." Wyatt settled his hands on Fiona's hips and positioned her in the middle of the room.

"Yes, Sir." Her response was breathy.

Wyatt slid her zipper down, teeth pulling apart one at a time, to expose her pale back. He slid his fingers under the straps and tugged them off her shoulders, letting the fabric fall to the ground in a circle around her feet. "You really aren't wearing anything else."

"I wouldn't make up something like that. How cruel," she said teasingly.

Parker moved as they did, to keep a good view. He was tempted to stroke himself through his jeans.

Wyatt looked her over, standing close but not making contact. "I was so wrong."

"About what?" Fiona asked.

"About how stunning you are naked. I thought I knew, but I wasn't even close." He rested his palm on her neck, then glided it down her shoulder and over her breast, pausing to caresses and elicit a moan before dropping his hand away.

Fiona raised her eyebrows. "Are we going to

just stare at me all night?"

Wyatt threaded his fingers in her hair and tugged, drawing a sharp gasp.

Fiona stared at him, eyes wide and pupils dilated. Her lips were flushed, and her chest heaved with each breath.

"You promised to trust me." Wyatt's voice had shifted to forceful and commanding.

She flicked her tongue over her bottom lip. "I do."

In the bedroom. Parker would leave it implied. That was what everyone meant, and no way was he ruining this.

"Good girl." Wyatt slid his fingers between her legs. "*Fuck*, I love how wet you get."

"I've…" Whatever she meant to say faded into a groan. Wyatt stroked and teased. Parker knelt next to them—to see Wyatt's fingers slide inside her, then back up to stroke her clit.

Fiona rocked her hips in time to the attention, swaying on her feet. Her groans grew louder. That familiar noise that meant she was close to orgasm made Parker's dick twitch, wondering why it was still caged.

She cried out when she came, grinding into Wyatt's fingers until the sweet sounds she made faded into panting breaths.

Wyatt knotted his fingers in her hair again and crushed his mouth to hers. How was this so arousing to see? Parker itched to set down the camera and join in, but he also liked drawing out the anticipation.

Wyatt released Fiona, then moved behind her. He stripped off his shirt, folded it diagonally, and rolled it twice, before fitting it over her eyes and tying it in place. He grasped her fingers. "Follow me. Slowly. I won't let you trip."

"All right." She let him lead her to the edge of the bed.

"Kneel on all fours on the bed. Hands at the edge of the mattress," Wyatt ordered.

Fiona did, and he shifted her a few inches, looking satisfied when he finished. He stepped back and looked at Parker. Wyatt pressed a finger to his lips, indicating they should be quiet.

Time ticked away, the silence growing heavy in the room. If this was tough on Parker, how did Fiona feel?

It was delicious.

"Hello?" she asked, her voice tiny.

"No talking." Wyatt slapped her ass, leaving a pink mark.

Fiona gasped.

The sharp sound left a ringing in Parker's ears after it faded.

When Wyatt reached around to hit *Stop* on the camera, it startled Parker. He'd almost forgotten he was part of this. Wyatt took the device away, set it aside, and pressed his body to Parker's. "I want to see you fuck her face," he whispered, as he slid down Parker's zipper. His fingers around Parker's cock were electric. With the buildup, it almost made Parker come.

Any doubts Parker had about this affair vanished in a haze of anticipation.

Chapter Fourteen

Fiona recognized Parker's scent. His rough grip as he tugged her hair and pushed her down. And his taste when he thrust in her mouth. He hit the back of her throat with the head of his cock, and she had to focus, to keep from gagging.

She could stop this if she wanted. There was no doubt in her mind. But having her sight gone and being on display between these two was a new kind of high, and she wasn't ready to come down.

Parker drove against her face. It was familiar and foreign at the same time, with these new restrictions in place. She wanted to reach between her legs and finger herself, but his intense pounding meant she needed both hands to keep herself upright.

Something nudged her opening. *Wyatt.* When he slid inside her, she groaned against Parker's shaft. Wyatt's movements were slower. More controlled. The mismatched pace set her brain off kilter.

Wyatt found her swollen clit and stroked gently. It was almost too much against the still-tender nub, but he kept his touch light. Being caught in the middle, being used and attended to at the same time, pushed her to the edge of climax, but Wyatt eased off each time she was right there. It was incredible and terrifying, how in-tune he was with her.

When he finally let her come, she wanted to scream. It was nearly impossible to do with Parker in her mouth.

Wyatt eased up on her sex but increased his pace. She clenched around him, riding the edge between too much and not enough. He gripped her hips hard, and she recognized his grunts. The staccato sound of him drawing close. Of his orgasm. The frantic pounding that accompanied it.

Parker slid from her mouth, startling her, and a spurt of warm and sticky cum hit her face.

Wyatt slowed to a stop but didn't pull out. He yanked her head back and pressed his chest to her back. "Do you want one more?"

She wasn't sure her legs would hold her up. She also couldn't find her voice, to answer.

"Later, then." Wyatt kissed down her spine, then slid out of her. He helped her to shift and sit on the mattress.

Her limbs were heavy, refusing to move, and a heady buzz hummed in her skull. Fiona couldn't think. She wanted to wrap herself in this cloud and stay for a while.

The blindfold fell away. Despite the gentle lighting, she blinked several times as her eyes adjusted.

"I think your shirt is ruined." Parker handed it to Wyatt.

"Doesn't matter."

Parker kissed Fiona's fingertips. "Be right back." He returned a moment later with a washcloth, and was tender as he washed away the physical evidence of the evening. He left and returned a second time, and handed her his shirt.

She pulled it over her head, sinking into his familiar scent and the soft fabric. Her every nerve ending was supercharged. Each sensation was amplified.

They drifted into friendly conversation, but she had a hard time focusing. She recognized enough to be happy Parker and Wyatt were getting along. They watched a movie, but she couldn't climb out of her own head.

Sitting with Wyatt behind her and Parker next to her felt so right. She wasn't supposed to trust Wyatt—she *knew* that—but she'd never felt safer. Wyatt's breath on the back of her neck and Parker's fingers tangled with hers were more comforting than she thought possible.

Fiona was supposed to be using this as a chance to get Wyatt out of her system, but she couldn't. The realization was terrifying. She wanted them both— Parker and Wyatt. Shouldn't have to choose. There was no desire for a random third person or experimenting with strangers.

She didn't see any way that this desire ended well. For any of them.

❤❤❤

Wyatt was dragged toward consciousness by Fiona's whimpers. His half-awake mind registered the terror in the sound, but he couldn't claw past sleep to investigate.

He hovered on that edge, as the mattress shifted. He forced himself awake at the sound of the balcony door sliding open and closing again, and opened his eyes to see Fiona silhouetted by the moonlight. Parker's shirt hung past her ass, leaving her barely decent.

A pang of concern spiked inside, as he put together the pieces of what woke him. He climbed from the bed.

"Don't go out there." Parker's voice startled him.

Irritation grew inside, and Wyatt turned to him. "She was crying in her sleep."

The only light in the room was what filtered in from outside and under the door. It let him see Parker scrub his face and sit with his back against the headboard. "She does that a lot," Parker said.

"What?" Wyatt's annoyance tilted toward anger.

"First several times, I joined her," Parker said. He sounded tired, and not just because it was the middle of the night. This was more of an exhausted-soul type of sound. "She's asked me to leave her alone until she's ready to talk."

Wyatt didn't like the sound of the request. Of leaving her alone when she was upset. "Is that smart?"

"It's what Fiona says she needs. I believe her, and it's not my place to tell her otherwise."

And that was one of the big differences between Parker and himself. Wyatt would push until he was certain she was taken care of. He didn't like his flash of doubt, asking if he was the one in the right.

"It was getting better, but the last three nights…" Parker trailed off.

Which meant it started on the night of the bombing. "I'm sorry." He pulled a chair out from the desk and sat facing Parker. It was odd, talking with both of them in their underwear and nothing else, but it wasn't uncomfortable. "So you sit up until she comes back in?"

"She gives me space while I live stream. Keeps quiet when I do interviews. Arranges her work schedule to let me see a new city every few days. The least I can do in return is wait up until she's ready to be around people again, when she gets stuck in nightmares about what happened with Tim."

Wyatt's envy mixed with anger. He tried to ball it up into a less potent cocktail, but it singed his thoughts. "I've given you a lot of shit about your relationship with Fiona, but the two of you are lucky." He meant it to be a throw-away comment, but the reality of it pressed in on him.

"Yeah. Pretty much."

Wyatt didn't want to dive into any conversation with depth. Didn't want to form any sort of bond with Parker. "How'd you get into Queensrÿche?"

Parker let out a long sigh. "I had a high school teach who was a fan. Introduced me to storytelling through mediums outside of books."

"And from there, it was a hop, skip, and jump to video blogging?"

"Lucky guess." Parker's chuckle sounded forced. "How do you do that?"

"You'll have to be more specific."

"Coax personal information from me without revealing anything about yourself."

"Fiona sees through me." Wyatt suppressed a cringe at the non-answer and the truth behind it.

"And I rarely see the world through her eyes. I get it—you're in sales. It's your job to milk the client. But who are you?"

Wow, that was a loaded question. Wyatt swallowed back the impulse that was always there. The one that insisted the answer was, *whoever you need me to be, until I get what I want and move on.* "Are you sure she's all right?"

"Nice redirect." A hint of disgust lined Parker's reply. "If you don't think I'm watching her closely, you're not paying attention."

"You really love her." The air conditioner kicked on, the hum threading with Wyatt's voice and buzzing in his ears.

"You knew that. Supposedly before I did. How did you turn this back on me? That's a neat trick."

"One you know. I've seen you employ it in your videos. Besides, you've caught more glimpses of me than most people ever do. What do you want to know?"

Parker scooted to the edge of the bed and swung his legs over, which put him only a few inches away. "Why the cathedral?"

"I like the artwork." Wyatt had the canned response without having to think.

Parker raised an eyebrow. "No stories about a tortured past in a private school?"

No, to any of the above. "Everybody's looking

for something to believe in. I'm no different. I used to go there when I was trying to find my faith. I was raised Catholic, but the only dark and dreary thing to come from that is I don't have a fetish for school-girl uniforms."

"And you're diverting the conversation again."

So much for staying away from the serious stuff. "My faith wasn't there or anywhere else I looked, and I accepted it. Now I like it for the art and the reminder of that revelation."

"So you do have a deep side." Fiona's voice startled him.

Parker must have seen her come in. How much did she hear?

How much did Wyatt want her to hear? He twisted to face her. "Surprised?"

"Only that you let it show," Parker said, at the same time Fiona replied, "No."

He liked both answers.

"Your phone's been going nuts for about ten minutes." Fiona nodded at the device where it sat on the dresser. "The light reflects on the glass each time it goes off."

Wyatt would deal with it in a moment. A short one, since anything worth calling him about at two-thirty in the morning had to be critical, but this was more so. "Are you all right?"

She sat next to Parker and pulled his arm around her. "I will be. See what's so important."

As Wyatt scrolled through several text messages from work, then listened to the voicemail, the probing conversation faded away in a fog of worry and disgust.

"What's wrong?" Parker asked.

"Another package bomb went off. Locally."

"*Jesus.*" Fiona's shock matched his.

"It was a few hours ago, and on the truck. Small enough the driver is okay and no one was hurt. But they found a second one on a different truck."

"Where was it going?" Fiona asked.

Odd question. "I don't know. Anyway, I have to take a raincheck on tomorrow." Later today? "Marketing and sales have to work on how we're spinning this. *Fuck*, that sounds cold. I hate this." He stopped himself before he could spill his thoughts. He'd rather tell everyone the truth about the situation. That wasn't like him.

"We'll let you work"—Fiona managed to dig up her dress and replace Parker's shirt with it without exposing herself—"but neither of us is going back to sleep anytime soon, so if you need anything…"

He should be making that offer to the woman who woke up in his bed terrified of a ghost that wouldn't stop haunting her. "Thanks."

She kissed him—a quick brush across the lips, but as distracting as anything they'd shared before. "Good luck," she said.

Wyatt dropped back into his chair after she and Parker left, and struggled to rope in his thoughts from every corner of his mind. He needed to focus on this bombing. He needed to not be thinking about the future—or lack thereof—with Fiona and Parker.

And he needed to figure out why the fuck he was so out of control these days. Before it destroyed his career and him.

Chapter Fifteen

Waking up and thinking she was in Tim's room, bound and helpless, always stole Fiona's thoughts and squeezed her chest until she couldn't breathe.

The terror faded each time she realized she was next to Parker. Tonight was no different. She still needed to clear her head, though. To put herself in a place where she *knew* Tim wasn't a threat anymore.

Coming back in to Wyatt and Parker talking was surreal—stepping into another dream. One she didn't mind.

Until the news about the next bombing hit Wyatt's phone.

Her calm was shattered. A buzz she couldn't name or shake lingered in her head. Sleep wouldn't be her friend tonight.

She and Parker reached their room, and he unlocked the door. "What now?" he asked. "Movies? Ungodly-late pizza? Ungodly-early breakfast?"

"None of the above." She grabbed her phone

and sent a quick text to Nick. *When you see the news, we're fine.* So he didn't freak out on her for not checking in. She dropped the device back in her purse, then sank onto the couch. "I was hoping we could sit. Talk. Not like a *we need to talk* kind of thing." Sort of, but not quite. "I just mean enjoy each other's company."

"Sure." He settled next to her.

She fiddled with the edges of the cushion and stared at her knees. "I was thinking about something on the balcony, and with the news, it might not be the best timing—"

"The timing is fine. The news was horrific, but no one was hurt. We're not putting anything off by letting it go on in the background. What's up?"

Now that the opportunity was there, the words wouldn't come. Or rather, everything that popped into her head sounded ridiculous. If Parker was okay with it, she wanted to add Wyatt to their relationship long term, but Wyatt had to want that too, and she wasn't convinced he did. And she still didn't trust him enough to think asking him would get her an honest answer.

So she could say, *Let's see where things go with all three of us*, but that was what they were doing.

"Red? What's up?" Parker lifted her chin, to look her in the eye.

"Thank you. For everything." It was the best she could come up with and didn't come close to what she wanted to say.

He smiled. "We do for each other. It's why we work together."

"I'm still grateful."

"I meant everything I said about Wyatt. I'm not just tolerating this. Tonight was fun, and it might have been even without the sex."

Relief that he almost read her mind trickled through her. It was close to the answer she wanted. She lay down on the couch and rested her head on his leg. "Movies sound good."

"Movies it is." He flipped on the TV, trailing his fingers through her hair with his free hand.

Fiona didn't realize she'd fallen asleep, until Parker's, "*God damn it*," jarred her awake.

She jolted up, heart hammering and pulse roaring in her ears. "What's wrong?" The question tumbled out before she finished processing her surroundings.

"Ms. Passion is about half a step from fucking doxing you. Also, call Nick." He was sitting at the table in the main room, laptop in front of him.

If his tone didn't drag her toward alertness faster than a shot of espresso, his words would have. "Wait. Back up. She what?"

He sighed and turned the laptop toward her. A few clicks later, the vlogger's smug face filled the screen. "My heart goes out to the affected families in these tragic bombings." Ms. Passion's tone was kind. Almost sympathetic. Who knew she had it in her? "I'm grateful no one was hurt in the most recent incident and hope the police bring those responsible to justice quickly."

Okay. That didn't sound so bad. Fiona couldn't swallow past the sick pit in her gut, though. Parker wouldn't be upset over this.

"However, I also hope that in their questioning,

they measure each person's answers carefully. I have it from a reliable source that they spoke to Fiona Walters in the last city, and are interested in doing so again this time. After she put an innocent man behind bars for her boyfriend's—"

Parker slammed the laptop shut, but the noise barely carried past the hammering of Fiona's pulse in her ears. "What did I ever do to her?"

"I wish I knew." Parker moved back to sit next to her. "I'd show you Wyatt's press release—all the news stations are playing it—but it's standard lip service, and he looks miserable. That might not cheer you up."

Fiona fell sideways and landed with her head against Parker's shoulder. "No. It probably wouldn't. You talked to Nick?"

"Yeah. He called a couple of hours ago."

How long did she sleep? She grabbed her phone. It was almost ten in the morning. She scrolled through the texts from her brother. The first one was sweet enough.

Thanks for letting me know. Give me a call when you're up.

The next one cranked her fury from *simmering* to *white-hot.*

What the fuck are you doing in the same city as Wyatt? Again?

She wasn't in the mood for Nick's holier-than-thou attitude. She stabbed out a reply.

Couldn't tell you. Maybe he's here because he works for the same company who hired us.

She'd call Nick back later. Once she had a chance to vent and rage and calm down a little. She had a missed call from an unknown number as well, along with a voicemail.

"Let's take off for the day." Parker's soft voice startled her. "Drive to a new town. Get away. Pretend nothing else exists."

Fiona should be irritated with him for suggesting they run away. But it was only temporary, and it sounded like the most brilliant idea she'd ever heard. "Let me see who this call is from first."

She pulled up the message and hit *Play*.

"Fiona, this is Martin Landry, with the FBI. I got your information from Detective Marshall in New Orleans. We'd like to speak with you."

Her gut turned in on itself, and she dropped her phone.

Fuck this. Fuck it all.

Fiona was tempted to crack a joke—ask if she could get a frequent-visitor punch card, for visiting police stations. Free cushioned seat on her next visit, maybe?

The expression on Agent Landry's face implied he wouldn't be amused. Possibly by anything. Ever.

"I'd like you to take a look at these." He slid three pieces of paper across the metal table they sat at.

She turned the printed photos to face her, and when pictures of herself stared back, her stomach dropped into her shoes. They were images of her from the trip to the vineyard. How did he get these? Why did they exist? "I'm looking."

"Do you recognize them?"

"Not these shots specifically. I know where I was when they were taken. We were at a winery near Philadelphia. The video of it is on Parker's channel."

Landry's frown deepened—she didn't think that was possible—and he drummed his fingers on the table. "Parker? Your boyfriend with the videos?"

"Yes."

"Could these have come from those?"

"Probably not. The lighting is wrong. They're taken from too far away. He and I stayed close most of the tour."

"I see." His tone didn't give anything away. "Did you have anyone else with you, taking pictures or doing any type of second-camera-angle filming?"

"No. Definitely not. Parker's a single-man operation." Should she mention Wyatt? Not unless the questions led there. He wasn't involved in this, and delving into why he'd been with them that day could damage both his and her career. "Where did you get them?"

He took the photos and placed them in a Manila folder. "I can't disclose that information at this time. Do you have any other thoughts of who might have taken these?"

"Tim." The answer came before she realized why.

"The man who was arrested for stalking and assaulting you?"

She nodded. Unlike last time, she refused to let this get to her. It wouldn't drill into her head and make her question how many places Tim followed her that she didn't know about. "That trip was about the time he started getting more insistent with his messages. I don't know if he was there that day or not."

She hoped not. If it wasn't Tim, where did the photos come from?

Ms. Passion's words echoed in her head, accusing Fiona of making the whole thing up for publicity. Memories of Tim forcing her into his room, binding her, and refusing to let her go were more vivid than she could stand.

What if Fiona had missed something else?

"I need you to take a look at these next." Landry handed her more photos.

She braced herself for another round of images of her that shouldn't exist. There was a wash of relief when she saw the grainy photos. As though they'd been taken from a security camera. The man in the image was dark haired, wore a suit, and stood at a convenience-store counter.

"Do you know this man?" Landry asked.

The guy could be anyone. His back was to the camera, and the quality was low, so no details stood out. "No."

"How about this man? Do you know him?"

Fiona's pulse sidestepped and kickstarted again at the photo of Wyatt. Why were they asking about him? "Of course. Wyatt Lindberg was my initial contact for the current project I'm working on. It looked like his handwriting on my business card—I told the detective that—and Wyatt and I have spoken several times over the past couple of weeks."

Agent Landry blinked, but there was no other shift in his expression. The man was probably a brutal poker player. "Has he ever followed you?"

"No." Well, there was that time he nicked their travel plans from Grammie's and used them to rearrange his schedule and meet them at the airport.

"Does he act odd or creepy around you?"

A lot of Wyatt's behavior would be creepy if she wasn't attracted to him. That was where that whole *consent* thing she'd tried to explain to Tim came into play. "No. Never."

"Are you sure?" Landry asked. The doubt that whispered across his face vanished quickly, but the break in his mask bothered Fiona.

"I'm absolutely sure. And I wouldn't hesitate to tell you otherwise if that were the case." She didn't like where the questions were headed.

"Where were you last night?"

She refused to get whiplash from the rapid shift in subjects. "Funny you should ask. Wyatt took Parker and me out, to see the town. A little vendor hospitality."

"What time did you go your separate ways at the end of the night?"

Fiona stalled. Not long, but she prayed the second's pause didn't show. "Late. I don't remember."

"Before midnight? After?" His tone grew more insistent.

Wyatt didn't do whatever Landry thought he did. He might be a manipulative fucker, but he wasn't a criminal. She could provide an alibi if needed, but she prayed it didn't come to that. For now, she'd make sure she didn't get him in hot water when he didn't need to be. "It was late. That's all I know."

This was nothing. Standard questioning, right? The warning bells going off in her head—concern for Wyatt—were because she'd seen too many crime dramas on TV.

Please let that be the case.

Chapter Sixteen

Irritation roared through Parker. He needed to get back inside the police station, to be there when Fiona finished, but the people in the lobby wouldn't appreciate overhearing his conversation.

"So, because Ms. Passion just strongly implied Fiona was here, rather than outright saying so, it's okay?" He wouldn't yell at Chloe. She was doing her job. She'd been kind enough to take his call. Her company had a lucrative business relationship with Fiona's.

He wouldn't yell, but he desperately wanted to.

"I know, and I'm sorry." Chloe sounded sincere. "She's been warned. She's fantastic at finding the loopholes."

Because how else would someone get away with making video reviews of sex toys that weren't labeled as *adult content?*

"What are we supposed to do?" He was asking himself more than her.

Chloe sighed. "I shouldn't be talking to you like

this. I should have sent you to the Support team."

"Then why'd you take my call?"

"For Fiona. Here's the honest deal—as much as I'm allowed to say, probably a little more than I should. This competition was a huge experiment for us. So many variables we didn't think would be a big deal. And we considered a lot. The tattoo artist in Italy? Tara? We're being sued because someone claims she used a dirty needle and gave them Hepatitis C."

"That sucks. For everyone." Parker didn't know what else to say. He also wasn't sure how it related to his situation, beyond being fucked up, but that would be rude to say.

Chloe gave a strained chuckle. "It does. My point is, we have to evaluate and see if this is profitable to do again, once we implement lessons learned."

"I hope you do. The bumps have sucked, but the opportunity… It's been incredible," Parker said.

"I'm glad. That's what I hoped for. Besides the fact that we got a dozen bloggers to promote us for free to their millions of subscribers."

Parker laughed. "Touché."

"But you're at that spot too." The seriousness returned to Chloe's voice. "Maybe it was a rhetorical question, but that's what you do now—you decide if you're still heading in a direction you want to be."

"Are you suggesting I quit if I don't like it?" When did he become beholden to a corporation's whims? He did the travel blog specifically to avoid that.

"Not at all. The intro on our website that says

we handpicked every contestant? I was the final sign-off. I loved what you did. I wanted you here."

"Thanks."

"And part of Ms. Passion's warning included probation. I shouldn't tell you this, but she has to run her live streams through us on a four-second delay, and if she does anything like this again, we pull her immediately."

That was something. "Then, thank you twice."

He disconnected with Chloe, but that didn't clear the conversation from his thoughts.

"Hey." Fiona wrapped her arms around his waist from behind and rested her cheek on his back. "Where's your head?"

"Everywhere." He covered her hands and leaned into the embrace. "How'd it go?"

"Better than last time, I think?"

That didn't sound promising. "Why the doubt?"

"They asked me a bunch of weird questions. A lot of them about Wyatt. Tell you about it over lunch?"

"Sounds good." And between now and when they reached their destination, maybe he could shake the question repeating in his head.

Was his career still heading in a direction he wanted?

Wyatt wasn't happy about working on a Sunday, especially since he needed to be in the office for his tasks. But most of his annoyance was directed at the *why* that had him here. The whole bombing thing… That the FBI and ATF were involved… That it spanned multiple states... That some dickless wonder had whatever manner of unresolved issues they thought could be fixed with blowing things up...

How long until someone was seriously injured? Killed?

His cellphone rang. Fiona's name on the screen blanketed his foul mood. "Hey, sexy lady."

"Hey, yourself. Is now a good time?" A strain ran through her voice.

He didn't blame her. "It's the perfect time. In fact, I need to take a break. Do you two want to meet somewhere? Coffee's on me."

"We'd love to." The lilt in her tone would have made him smile, if it weren't for the unspoken *but*.

"What's going on?"

She sighed. "It's why I'm calling. Meeting in person probably isn't the best idea."

His concern spiked. "Red? Talk to me."

"I spent the morning talking to the FBI. And I'm probably being paranoid telling you *no*, but they asked a lot of questions about you."

Ominous. "Like what?" He had some solidly bad memories about the last time the police took a personal interest in him.

"They asked if I knew you. If I was with you last night. I guess that's not a lot after all, but the questions didn't focus on anyone else."

He could let the idea take root and run away with his concern, but he didn't do *mindless panic*. However, this might be a good time to try out that whole opening-up thing. "I *did* use to have a criminal record." He kept his tone light.

Her laugh was filled with disbelief. "*Use to*? Is

this another *I got drunk at a frat party* story?"

He liked that she remembered the first one. "Not exactly." The words stuck when he realized what he was about to admit. "Promise me you won't freak out until you've heard the whole story."

"So… no, I can't promise that. But I will hear you out." The amusement was gone from her voice.

"I say *I used to* because the record was expunged after I served my probation. And I wasn't guilty, but I was young and was convinced pleading down was better than going to trial and risking losing."

"You don't want to tell me." Was that accusation?

He twisted his mouth. "I do." But he was scared of her reaction. The realization left a bad taste in his mouth. Things like that didn't scare him. He stowed the weak reaction. "I was charged as an accomplice to felony stalking and assault."

"That's what Tim is charged with." Her tone was unreadable.

"It is. But in my case it was several counts, and most of them were worse."

"I see."

He wished he could watch her face.

"I promised to hear you out," she said. "Why *accomplice*?"

"I was dating a guy…" He'd told Parker this story but left out the details. Delving deeper into his own naïveté was going to suck. "Open relationship. We liked variety."

Fiona snorted. "You? Can't imagine."

He let the sarcasm slide. Six months ago, it was

still true. Now? His tastes had become distinctly focused. "We'd help each other pick up girls in bars. One of us would be the unwanted creep, and the other would sweep in as her knight in shining armor and *save* her."

"That's tacky." Emotion bled into her voice, raw and tinged with disgust.

"It was. I'm falling back on the *I was young and didn't know better* excuse. If he was interested, I'd crank up the overbearing, aggressive asshole to an eleven. If he was helping me, he'd be clingy and sweet and rattle on about how more girls should give the nice guy a chance. I'd step in and be confident and *scare* him off."

"Tacky with an extra side of gross. You could have—you know—stood on your own merits, rather than being the less disgusting choice in a shitshow taste test."

"Ouch. But fair. I'd like to pretend I was never that guy, but I was, and I'd rather you know."

"Why?"

"Your opinion matters to me." That was on odd thing to confess. Typically only the clients' opinions mattered, and only until they signed the contract. "What you said the other day, about wanting to be seen for what's under the surface? I don't ever want that. With anyone. Or I didn't, until you and Parker."

When she chuckled, it was dry, but the harshness was gone from it. "You still haven't explained the police record."

"Right. I didn't realize it at the time, but that's what a lot of Devin's hookups became. If he ran into rejection before he was done having his fun, he turned obsessive. A couple of accusations came back to me, because I was the person the women remembered as the asshole. My… preferences made me easy to profile. The guy who likes his girl tied up and begging must be the sick fuck doing the drugging and raping, right?" He winced at the bitterness that slipped out.

She sighed.

He waited for more. "What are you thinking?" he prompted when she didn't say anything.

"I can't see it. Not from you."

The basic assurance nudged away some of the cloud inside. "So they arrested me, I figured out what Devin had been up to, my testimony got him put away for several years, and I already explained the rest."

"I believe you."

Ego insisted that of course she did. It was the truth. Experience said that didn't always matter. "Thanks. So… no dinner?"

"It's not good idea." Her disappointment was almost tangible. "I'm worried that, if the police keep bringing me in for questioning, that will lead to needing to prove alibis, and that will hurt us both."

"I wish I didn't understand, but I do. I'll show you a night you'll never forget, once this is wrapped up."

"You always do. Talk to you at work?"

"Yeah."

As Wyatt disconnected, mixed emotions raged inside. He liked opening up more than he should have. But having to keep his distance from Fiona and Parker didn't sit well with him.

Nothing to do for that. He dove back into his work, grateful for the distraction, despite hating the bombings.

He'd been working for another hour or so, when his cellphone rang again. He didn't recognize the number, beyond know it was from out of state. "This is Wyatt Lindberg."

"Mr. Lindberg, this is Agent Landry, Federal Bureau of Investigation. I'd like to sit down with you face to face, and ask you some questions."

Logic said that asking if he needed a lawyer would make him look guilty. Experience pointed out that didn't matter. "Should I bring my attorney?"

The silence that followed wasn't reassuring.

"You're not being charged at this time, but I'm required to tell you that yes, should you want one present, it would be advised," Landry said.

Wyatt clenched his fist until his knuckles ached. He had no idea why this was falling back on him. Maybe it wasn't, and Fiona read the situation wrong. Either way, he refused to let things go down like last time. "I understand. Let me get a hold of him. Then, we'll talk."

<h1>Chapter Seventeen</h1>

Wyatt didn't like the clawing inside, as he and his attorney sat across from Agent Landry in a small box of a room. He didn't care for the memories associated with this. But he wasn't that naive guy anymore, and he didn't break anymore.

He had this under control.

Charles Martin was a friend of a colleague, and seemed like a professional, collected lawyer. Wyatt was supposed to nudge Charles's shoe if he wanted the questioning to stop.

It wouldn't be an issue, because Wyatt hadn't done anything. The thought echoed one he had so long ago, and would have made him snort at his own ignorance under difference circumstances.

"Do you recognize this convenience store?" Agent Landry showed him a printed photo he pulled from what appeared to be a folder full of them.

Wyatt nodded. "It's a few blocks from the home offices, in Atlanta. I'm in there a couple times a week, when I'm not traveling."

"Have you ever purchased a prepaid debit card there?"

"A what? You mean those Visa gift cards? They make good gifts." Wyatt should be able to figure out where the conversation was headed, even with so few questions. He didn't have any guesses. He tucked away his concerns.

Agent Landry scribbled on the pad in front of him. From where Wyatt sat, it didn't appear to be more than random scuffs with the pen on paper. "Is that a *yes*?" Landry asked.

"Yes."

"Have you ever purchased a prepaid cell phone?"

Wyatt resisted the desire to shift in his seat. The metal frame wasn't that uncomfortable; the situation just made him think it was. "Not anytime in the last decade."

"I see." Landry pulled another sheet from his folder and showed it to Wyatt. "Do you recognize this?"

It was Fiona. From the background, it looked like it was taken in the vineyard they'd visited. And he certainly remembered that dress and what she hadn't been wearing underneath it. "I know who it is. Fiona Walters is the implementation resource for a vendor we're working with."

"Do you recognize where it was taken?"

The answer stuck in Wyatt's throat. How much could he say? It was hard to know, without having an idea why they were asking.

Charles cleared his throat, and Wyatt gave a slight shake of his head. He grabbed the photo and squinted. "Hard to tell with the low resolution. The wine bottles make me think… in a place that sells wine?"

"Have you ever visited the vineyards in Chadds Ford, Pennsylvania?" Agent Landry had to be one hell of a poker player. If Wyatt weren't inching toward concern for his future, he'd buy the guy a beer and ask how he kept such an impassive mask in place.

"I have. There's a stunning place out there I drop by when I'm visiting their local offices. The owner is friendly, and the wine is good." The owner who he'd personally pulled strings with, to let Parker film there. Fuck. A few pieces tumbled into place.

Landry slid the image back into his folder. "When was the last time you visited?"

This was a bad direction for the conversation to go. Not because Wyatt was worried about his guilt, but he couldn't damage Fiona's career. The vehemence of the thought caught him off-guard. "I suppose one of the last times I was in Philadelphia."

"Were you there with Ms. Walters?"

Wyatt nudged Charles' foot. He'd deflect for himself all day long, but he wouldn't hang Fiona out. Especially for something she didn't know at the time.

"We're done with the questions," Charles said.

"The vineyard owner remembers the last time you were there." Apparently, Landry wasn't. "Acting as a tour guide for Ms. Walters and her boyfriend, while he filmed for his YouTube channel?"

"We're not answering anything else." Charles's tone was firm.

Wyatt kept his expression blank, mirroring

Landry's. He didn't like the chaos that bubbled inside. This was making him look guilty. He didn't know if admitting where he'd been would add fuel to whatever Landry thought he had.

"According to your company's records, as well as hers, she wasn't in communication with you at that point as a vendor." Landry had another fucking photo of Fiona. "Do you recognize this one?"

Wyatt didn't have to squint or guess. The stained glass in the background was from the cathedral he'd taken them to. Where the hell did these images come from? They weren't the right angle to be Parker's, and they were distinctly only of Fiona. No other people in the background. He kept his mouth shut. They'd passed the point where he could say anything.

"What kind of deal did you negotiate, to have your felonies stricken from your record?" Landry asked.

Wyatt's mask almost slipped.

"*Stricken from the record* means they no longer exist. Felony expunging is common so many years after the sentence has been served." Charles stood. "I don't know what you misunderstood about *no more questions.*"

"How about I offer a little information, then you do the same?" Landry's tone shifted to conversational. Wyatt was impressed. The guy would make a hell of a salesman. "The photos are from a memory card we found in a pre-paid cell phone, which was in the box containing the unexploded device. The fingerprints on the card match those on file with an arrest record from more than a decade ago, belonging to Wyatt Lindberg. The phone was purchased at the convenience store in Atlanta. The shipping slips were purchased on local networks with the company, using a prepaid card purchased at the same store."

Well, fuck.

"All circumstantial." Charles didn't hesitate.

Landry shook his head. "Except the fingerprints. And the several eye-witness reports placing Mr. Lindberg where he didn't need to be. The statement from a Grammie's Administrative Assistant, that Wyatt went out of his way to grab Fiona's schedule long before she had anything to do with his employer. The lack of his alibis. The previous conviction—"

"Which is inadmissible, since it no longer exists." Charles's voice was tight.

It didn't matter. Wyatt's future had flashed before his eyes, and it was a repeat of the last time he was arrested. He had no idea where this all came from. Tim? The photos maybe, but not the memory card. Or the bombs.

This was so very bad.

Parker kept half an eye on his camera and the rest of his attention on Fiona, as they strolled through the outdoor mall someone had recommended. He had to get his filming hours in, but he wasn't feeling it.

"Ooh, I love these." Fiona tugged him toward a boutique with a table of hats out front.

He wanted to give her his focus. He wanted to not have to stick to a schedule. He didn't want to be the spoiled child, who complained about the fact that his self-made job was requiring a little discipline.

"What do you think?" Fiona wore a hat with a broad brim, in a green that matched her eyes.

Her smile drew one from him. "I'm biased. I think you're stunning regardless."

"Fair point." She set the hat back with the others, then kissed him on the cheek. "You lead, I'll follow. Where do you need to be?"

Here. With her. He wouldn't mind if Wyatt were here, too. It was a sentiment he didn't like understanding, but the more time they spent with Wyatt, the more Parker liked him. It wasn't the same trying not to fall and failing that Fiona struggled with, but the friendship was growing. Parker liked hanging out with him. Partly because it made Fiona happy, but there was more to it.

A month ago, Parker would have sworn that would never happen.

"Handmade candy?" Fiona asked.

"No. *God*, no. I never thought I'd get sick of seeing someone pull taffy, but seriously."

She nodded toward a park that sat at the end of the street. "Peace Gardens?"

"Perfect." He followed her, keeping the camera trained anywhere else. He wanted to film her. Capture each smile and laugh when she pointed something out or tried another thing on. He also wanted to put the camera down until there was footage worth recording, and join her in appreciating their surroundings without a lens in the way.

She tangled her fingers in his and stepped in his path, stopping him. "You look miserable."

"I'm fine."

"Which is bullshit, and we both know it."

He let out a flat chuckle. "Okay. I'm not. But it's a lot to put into words all at once."

"I get it. Or I can make a couple of educated guesses." She pressed closer until her body molded to his, and held his gaze. "Advice a friend gave me a few months back, adapted for the now. If you could be doing anything, right this very minute, and not have to worry about obligation, what would it be?"

He recognized that question. It was the logic he'd used to persuade her to come on this trip. "This." He circled an arm around her waist and kissed her.

She draped her arms around his neck and yielded to the hungry press of his lips. Her sigh was tantalizing, and she tasted like coffee and mint.

He broke away reluctantly but didn't let her go. "Beyond that? I don't know. I want to have fun. See everything. Not be tied to a production clock."

"So do it." She snagged his camera before he realized what she was up to, and skipped ahead. "Go mingle. Talk to these people. Be the charismatic guy who landed a spot in this competition to begin with. I'll be an extension of your arm."

He grasped her wrist and pulled her back to him. Fingers covering hers, he slid her hand down to his jeans, to cup his shaft. "If you're acting as an extension of my arm, I've got a different suggestion."

"Earn it." She twisted away with a playful smirk.

"Excuse me?"

"I'm still making you do your job. Go be the

Parker your viewers love. Have fun. And then you can use my hand however you'd like."

It was silly. It was simple. And for the next couple of hours, it was the most fun he'd had filming, in ages.

The sun was dipping below the horizon, and he was debating if he had enough footage to cut into a video, when Fiona said, "Hang on. Text from Nick."

She handed Parker's camera back, then read the message aloud. "If you're not ignoring me, get current on the bombing news, then call me."

"That sounds ominous." Parker led her out of the flow of foot traffic, while she jabbed her phone screen.

"The headlines say they arrested someone." She scanned the display as she spoke. "No names are being released at this time, but the police will be holding a press conference later, and they're glad they brought the suspect in so quickly."

That sounded like a good thing, which didn't explain the twisting in his gut.

"I'm calling Nick." She held the phone to her ear. Her half of the conversation was brief, but as she listened, her face went pale. "I'm here. Call me with whatever you need me to do… I will be. Talk to you soon."

She dropped the device in her purse and turned a blank stare on Parker.

"What's wrong?" he asked.

"The shipping company is putting our implementation on hold. It's not a *cancel*, but it is for an undetermined amount of time. They'll pay my expenses and cover any costs associated with the reschedule." She frowned.

"That's not what's wrong." The gnawing inside grew.

"They're figuring out how to frame things for the public. Getting statements ready for when the full story hits the media. Preparing for the backlash."

"Fiona? Details." Though he wasn't sure he needed to hear them.

She finally focused on him. "Wyatt's the suspect they arrested."

Chapter Eighteen

Fiona wished she could be numb—send a rush of ice through her veins and put a halt to everything she felt. She couldn't stop worrying about Wyatt. About whether or not she'd said something that led to his arrest. About the fact that the real bomber was still out there.

She should be focused on things she should control. Would this delay hurt them? Could she meet her development deadline with so much going on in her head?

No matter which angle she approached things from, her thoughts came back to Wyatt.

She couldn't go visit him, for the sake of their jobs. There was no way to find out what was really going on. Did he have family this was about to unleash hell on? She wasn't worried about a wife or a girlfriend. Maybe she should be, but this stupid trust of hers had a long reach. Siblings, though? Friends? Parker and Nick would rain fury down if she was the one in jail.

Wyatt would too.

Fiona was supposed to be working on that deadline, while Parker did edits and voice-over in the other room. Instead, she was refreshing the news on her laptop. Every five seconds, she told herself *this is the last time* and looked to see if there was any new information about the arrest.

Refresh.

The clock told her she'd been at it for more than an hour.

Refresh.

This couldn't be healthy.

Refresh.

Did she care?

Refresh.

Bomber identity released.

Her stomach dropped into her shoes at the headline. It plummeted through the floor when she saw the video was Ms. Passion's, and despite being posted less than ten minutes ago, it had over a hundred-thousand views.

Fiona braced herself and clicked *Play*.

The standard intro ran, fading to show Ms. Passion leaning into the camera, her trademark conspiratorial expression in place. "Okay, I know y'all are sick of me talking about this, but I promise the reward is worth it, and after today, back to the toys."

The buildup cranked Fiona's tension higher with each filler word, until she thought her muscles might snap.

"...inside scoop for you. I know who they arrested in conjunction with the bombing. Before you ask, no I can't say. Protecting my sources and all."

"*Just get it over with*," Fiona shouted at her laptop.

"Red?" Parker was by her side in an instant.

"The FBI arrested Fiona Walters—"

"*Fuck you*." Fiona didn't care that she was screaming. It was better than giving in to the desire to vomit.

Parker flipped the lid shut on her laptop and grabbed her phone. "Stop watching. It's not going to do you any good."

It would feed her rage and burn away the nausea. That sounded pretty good. *Shit*. Ms. Passion basically told the entire internet what city Fiona was in.

"…no, it's Parker…"

She was vaguely aware he was talking to someone on her phone.

"…Because there's a better chance you'll take her calls. I don't care if it didn't go through you. You know people over there. Get it pulled *now*." He sounded furious.

Fiona didn't blame him. She wanted to reach through the screen and strangle Ms. Passion. What the fuck was that woman's problem?

The snapping she'd feared severed her brain from her emotions. It was as though the adrenaline shut off access to that part of her, and nothingness sank in.

"No, it's not true. Why the fuck would you ask that?" Parker's voice grew louder. He handed her the phone.

Fiona didn't know who she was talking to. She

didn't care. "Hello?"

"Are you all right?" Chloe asked. "We're working right now to get that video pulled. He's right; we have contacts at YouTube."

"Awesome." Fiona couldn't find the enthusiasm to mean it. A beep sounded in her ear, and she glanced at the screen. "That's Nick. I gotta go." She swiped over to the new call, not hearing whatever Chloe said. "Hey." There was the numbness she wanted earlier.

"What's going on?" Nick sounded like he was on the verge of panic. "Who do I need to eviscerate?"

Huh. She'd been right. They did raise hell on her behalf. She felt like she'd been drugged or was watching this unfold through borrowed eyes. It wasn't real. It couldn't be. "I don't know who. I'm fine."

"You don't sound fine."

Parker took the phone from her again. She listened to him talk at Nick, but she didn't process the words. She couldn't make sense of any of it. Something about a hotel. A new one. Was Nick buying a hotel? That was silly. They wrote software for a living.

But a woman she didn't know risking her livelihood to accuse Fiona of a crime she didn't commit was just as ridiculous.

"I'll keep you updated," Parker said. "I promise. Call, send a carrier pigeon—anything, if you hear anything. We'll get back to you." Parker tossed her phone on the table next to her computer. "We need to pack."

"Why?" She looked up at him. The logic centers of her mind had stopped working. "She told everyone

I was arrested. They'll look for me in jail."

Parker knelt in front of her and cradled her cheeks in his hands. The warm pressure tugged at reason. "It won't take them long to figure out you're not the person in jail. This is already viral. Populating in trending headlines. *Everywhere.* Even if an apology goes out immediately—and I have no idea what the odds are there—a lot of people won't hear the retraction. And those who do will want to talk to you. The police aren't saying anything. The shipping company isn't saying anything. Answers are scarce, and you just became a person who might have them."

"Okay." That made sense. Why didn't she think of any of that? Why did this random stranger fuck Fiona over so hard? That question wouldn't stop repeating in her head.

Parker pulled her to her feet. "It's not a big deal. We'll pack, go to a new hotel, and lie low until this blows over."

She nodded. It wasn't as though they had a choice. Ms. Passion took that from them.

❤❤❤

Wyatt didn't like this feeling. This lack of control. This not knowing where to go next.

He wouldn't fidget, though. He didn't give into doubt. He paced in his hotel room because he was tired of being cooped up. At least he was here, and not still in a jail cell—the benefit of an expensive attorney, who pushed hard to get Wyatt released on bail.

He would put up with the low-end room and lack of amenities, if it meant a little more freedom until his arraignment.

The knock was a welcome distraction and kicked a new flavor of anticipation into his bloodstream. He probably wasn't supposed to have these guests, but since the judge didn't explicitly forbid it, Wyatt was taking his chances.

He let Fiona and Parker in. Before the door finished swinging shut behind them, he cupped Fiona's cheeks between his palms and crushed his mouth to hers.

Her gasp drove him to deepen the kiss. The way she fisted his shirt in her hands mirrored the desperation clawing inside him. He wanted to spin her away, press her against the wall, and drag her jeans down her legs, so he could slide inside her.

But the even stronger compulsion was to tug his guests into the room, and… cuddle in front of the TV? *Ridiculous.*

Parker clearing his throat threaded reason into Wyatt's thoughts. He broke away from Fiona, clasped Parker's hand, and gave him a half-hug.

"Prison make you lonely and desperate?" Parker teased.

Wyatt forced a chuckle. "Something like that." The jail-time part of his last forty-eight hours was the least of his concerns. He'd been stuck in a holding cell, where his glower earned him privacy. He knew why he was there and what was expected of him. "Charles told me what Ms. Passion did. How are you?"

They moved from the entryway into the room, but Wyatt was too wound up to sit.

Fiona's soft touch on his hand sent desire racing

across his skin. "Desperate for an outlet." Her voice was as demure as the way she watched him through her lashes, but the words screamed in his thoughts.

That initial impulse roared back, heat searing through his veins. "What did you have in mind?"

"Use me."

Two brief words. That was all it took to make him rock hard. He stepped back to stand next to Parker and said, "Take off your clothes."

Fiona shifted from shy to a vixen in a blink. She glided her hands up her sides, then back down, before slowly peeling off her T-shirt. The turquoise of her bra was vibrant against her porcelain skin and drew out the spark of mischief in her eyes.

She kicked off her sandals, then turned away. Her hips swayed to a beat only she heard. She bent at the waist, to slide her jeans down her legs and step out of them, presenting her ass, round and tight. A barely-there scrap of lace covered the temptation between her legs.

Parker's low groan matched Wyatt's thoughts. Wyatt had never seen a more erotic striptease. The *who* might have a little to do with it. Maybe.

Fiona whirled to face them again. She slid her bra straps down freckled arms, before reaching behind her to unclasp the hooks. The lingerie fell to the floor, leaving her full breasts on display, her nipples pink and erect and begging to be pinched.

Wyatt exercised restraint. She could tease for now, because he had wicked plans for when she was finished with the show.

She hooked her thumbs in the elastic of her panties and tugged them low, exposing a patch of smooth skin. She finally nudged the clothing down enough to let it fall away, leaving her naked.

A flush traveled across her skin as he looked her over. *Stunning.*

And it was his turn. He pulled out the wooden chair from the desk. "Sit."

Fiona raised her eyebrows.

He slapped her ass. The *crack* filled the room, adding fuel to the fire spilling inside him. "Each time I do that, it's going to make it tougher for you to sit comfortably. And I said *sit.*"

"For how long?" she asked.

He spanked her again, this time on the other cheek. Two pink spots reflected back at him. "Until I say you're done. Sit. Watch. Nothing but those two things. No talking. No moving. *No* touching. Anyone."

She bit her bottom lip and complied, sinking into the chair.

Wyatt turned his back to her. When he gripped the back of Parker's neck, Parker's eyes grew wide, but he didn't resist the kiss.

It was supposed to be as much for show as anything, but their lips met, and the need in Wyatt cranked another notch. A few more, and the switch would snap. Wyatt thrust his tongue into Parker's mouth. Desire was driven by both the physical contact and knowing Fiona watched, silently.

Parker pushed back, rather than away, raking his nails along Wyatt's chest. It was the same power struggle that always existed between them, but it was more.

"Too many clothes," Parker gasped when they

broke apart. He dragged down the front of Wyatt's shirt, undoing buttons along the way and popping at least two off.

It didn't matter. Wyatt yanked Parker's Tee off, needing to feel more skin.

He ground his erection into Parker's hip, barely aware he was humping.

Parker made quick work of Wyatt's zipper, and Wyatt returned the favor, not caring about the sound of fabric tearing.

Their clothes fell away far more quickly than Fiona's had. Wyatt gripped Parker's shaft and squeezed enough to draw a groan, before slowly stroking it.

Parker bit into his shoulder, then traveled his mouth along Wyatt's chest, sucking. Probably leaving marks.

Part of Wyatt wanted to force Parker to his knees. Feel Parker's mouth around his shaft.

Fiona whimpered, and Wyatt's focus narrowed to a point. This was for show. He wanted something else. He took one last, hungry kiss from Parker, before turning back to Fiona.

"Stand up," he ordered.

She did. Her chest heaved with each breath.

Wyatt approached her and glided two fingers between her legs, not making any other contact. She was slippery wet, and it was easy to dip inside her.

She clenched around him.

"You like that?" he asked.

The flush on her skin was a tantalizing shade of pink. "*God*, yes."

"If you're this turned on already, I could go back

to your boyfriend. Let you watch me finish him off."

Her pussy tightened around him again, but she didn't speak.

"Well?" Wyatt prompted.

"I'm deciding if I should give you an answer that will earn me another spanking, or if I should go with, *whatever you want*, to see what you have in store."

He did adore this woman. "What's your conclusion?"

"Whatever you want." She smirked.

He could slap her ass again. Instead, he plunged his fingers deeper inside her, drawing a sharp gasp. "*I want to watch the two of you fuck*," he said as he moved behind her. He kissed along her shoulder and withdrew from her. "I want to see you riding Parker." Wyatt slid a wet finger between her ass cheeks.

She groaned.

"And I'll decide what else I want from there." He nudged her puckered hole and slipped his finger inside. The sounds she made were like a good drug, feeding his high. With his other hand, he cupped her breast and kneaded, pinching and rolling her nipple.

She squirmed against him, short pants tearing from her throat.

He caught her earlobe between his teeth. "Do you trust me?"

"Always."

The word drilled into him, almost disrupting his arousal—it carried far more weight than it should. But he refused to read more into it. "Stop me if it's too much."

Chapter Nineteen

"It won't be." Every inch of Fiona's body was an erogenous zone. The sting in her ear, from Wyatt's bite, surged with the rest of her anticipation. She swore, if she squirmed at the right angle, she'd come.

Wyatt slid his touch away, and an ache for more grew inside her.

Parker grasped her hands and pulled her to him as he backed toward the bed. The way he watched her, with desire and love, buoyed her heart. He circled her waist with his arm and drew her in, to press his body to hers. The heat of his skin seared into her bones.

"You're incredible," he said, brushing a strand of hair from her forehead.

The words rolled through her. "Not without both of you." She didn't mean to admit that aloud.

Parker didn't look upset. He brushed his mouth over hers, then kissed along her jaw, following a random path to her breast. When he wrapped his mouth around one nipple and scraped his teeth over the tender skin, she arched her back.

He continued to suck and lick as he lowered himself onto the mattress, bringing her with him. She straddled his legs and leaned over, not wanting to surrender any contact.

The exchange was intimate. Erotic and safe. But knowing Wyatt watched it, standing just in view, slowly stroking himself, brought the encounter to a new level.

She reluctantly straightened, to lower herself onto Parker's shaft. He slid inside her, stretching her out and filling the spot Wyatt teased moments earlier. Parker's groans as she rode him ignited the air.

"*Fuck*, you two are sexy together." Wyatt's gravelly comment wove into the moment, rather than disrupting it.

Fiona liked this more than she thought possible. Being on display. Being part of… whatever this was. She was worried defining it would destroy it, but it was wicked and delicious and incredible.

Parker glided his palms up her stomach, grazing her breasts, before moving down to grip her hips. He dug his fingers into her pelvis and thrust up hard, setting a faster, more desperate pace.

Wyatt stepped behind her, his chest pressing into her back. He scraped his teeth over her shoulder and reached around her, to stroke her clit. The new contact was a jolt that traveled from her core, extending to her fingers, toes, and tongue.

His touch was light and coaxing. Combined with the way Parker slammed inside her, it pushed Fiona toward the edge of climax and sent her tumbling over in a heartbeat. Her heart was hammering fast.

She clenched around Parker as she came, not wanting to let go of the rush.

The sharpness of the orgasm dulled but didn't subside, as both men continued their attentions. Parker tightened his grip, and she knew he was close. His face screwed up, and he spilled inside her.

It took a moment for him to slow his pace, then come to a stop. She leaned her palms on his chest, grasping for her breath.

Wyatt placed his hand loosely on her throat, startling her and kickstarting a pulse just starting to slow. His breath was hot on her cheek. "You wanted to be used?"

She didn't know why she'd said that earlier, but the words tasted good then, and were like lightning in her veins now. "Yes."

"I want to fuck you while your boyfriend's cum is still dripping out of your tight, perfect pussy. On your back."

She moved to roll off Parker. Wyatt grabbed her shoulder and pushed her roughly, until she was lying down, looking up at him.

He pressed his hand to her throat again, gaze locked on hers.

She expected a little more verbal play. Another command or compliment.

He shoved her thighs apart with his knee, knelt between them, and thrust inside her with a single stroke, watching her. Where Parker studied her with affection, Wyatt's attention was dark and intense, but the adoration was still there.

The combination was alluring. It was also terrifying, because she would willingly drown in it.

She wrapped her legs around Wyatt's waist, wanting to be closer.

"Finger yourself." Wyatt's voice was a tight growl. "Make yourself come again."

Fiona lowered her hand as commanded, but she didn't know if she could comply with the rest of his order. The hyper-sensitive edge had dulled to a low thrum of pleasure. She hovered near climax, but it seemed out of reach.

Parker leaned in, to suck on her nipple again while he played with her other breast.

Orgasm built inside. A slow, sensual climb to the peak.

She squeezed her eyes shut when she came, and stars danced behind her eyelids. Wyatt pressed his palm into her windpipe, enough to make her air thin, but not cut it off. The lightheaded rush in her skull careened toward weightless. Ecstasy wrapped around her in a blanket, stealing thought away. She rode the high as far as she could.

In the background, she heard Wyatt's familiar grunts and knew he was coming too.

She slipped back into the now, but not completely, as he eased off the pressure on her throat.

Slowly, other sensation crept back in. Her neck was sore. Her pussy was sore. *God*, it felt incredible.

Wyatt slipped out of her and crawled up next to her on the bed. She was vaguely aware of him disposing of the condom, before he spooned into her. Parker lay on her other side, and she rested her head on his shoulder.

Exhaustion—some from the sex, and the rest from the release of tension—seeped into her. She wanted to curl into this moment and live here.

Parker trailed his fingers through her hair. "Watching the two of you together is as incredible as being a part of it. Different, but just as amazing."

"What he said." Wyatt's lips vibrated against the back of her neck. "Is this what you had in mind?"

She'd wanted new. Rough. Incredible. How much dirtier would he get next time, if she let him? "It's so much better."

"Good."

♥♥♥

Wyatt sat on the bed with Fiona and Parker, TV playing in the background. They weren't paying attention. They'd gotten dressed again, but part of Wyatt wished they hadn't.

He couldn't shake the looming fear that he had something incredible here and it was about to be ripped away.

Parker was catching Wyatt up on the competition. "They kicked Ms. Passion out, so the good news is, no elimination round this month." His laugh was forced. The competition wasn't a priority.

The way Fiona perched on the mattress, it looked like she might bolt any minute. So much for sex being a good stress outlet. "We got out before the press hounds uncovered our old room number. Another lesson learned from the Tim incident. No one knows where we're staying. For now."

Wyatt wasn't using his name on the registration either. Charles had secured the room under a satellite company his law firm used for cases like this, when clients needed to keep a low profile. Not that Wyatt could afford the firm's services much longer. His savings would deplete fast, especially now that he didn't have a paycheck coming in.

"What about you?" Parker asked.

"Where to start?" Wyatt let out a long breath. "The morality and public persona clause in my contract means I lost my job. I took out a hefty lien against my condo to pay my bond. And I'm not allowed to leave the state before my arraignment." He also had to check in with an agent every four hours, to verify he was still here. "So nothing too damning." He tried to keep his tone light.

Fiona frowned.

"I've been through worse." He didn't have as much to lose last time. He refused to let any of this get to him, though. Wyatt wouldn't let this break him.

"Did they tell you why they think it's you?" Even when her face was painted with concern, Fiona was impossible to take his eyes off.

He didn't like that either. He was spinning out of control with her. His sex life was the one place he should still have final say, and every step of the way, Fiona made him fumble. It was easy to pretend otherwise before, but now he couldn't ignore the way all these pieces snapped together in a broken puzzle. Whoever was behind the bombings, Wyatt, Fiona, and Parker wouldn't be involved if their lives hadn't intersected.

Wyatt repeated the details Landry gave him at the time of his arrest.

Parker's brows nearly reached his hairline. "So they think you mailed a bunch of bombs because you were following Fiona? How does that make sense?"

"I wish I knew. The evidence gets more damning, though. They found remnants of the supplies used to make the local devices. A specific type of wire that not many people sell. It was tucked inside the trash that came out of the hotel that day. Along with print-outs on company letterhead, that say how to make the bomb."

Fiona snorted. "They don't think very highly of your ability to cover your tracks if they think you left that all in such obvious places."

The comment almost drew a smile. He wanted to joke back about being a much more discreet bomber, but the jest fell flat before it finished forming.

"But you didn't do it." There was no doubt in Parker's voice. "You've got alibis. Travel schedules. All sorts of information to the contrary."

Wyatt tried to hide his wince. "Sort of."

"What does sort of…? Oh." Fiona's expression shifted to understanding. "The photos of me."

"Fuck." Parker sighed.

Exactly. Wyatt couldn't prove where he was half the time, because it was with Fiona and Parker.

"So I'll tell them where you were." Fiona sounded like the answer was simple.

Wyatt knew better. "No."

Parker pushed away from the wall. "You're going to pick now to care about her job? Lousy time to learn to be a good guy."

"Big surprise—I agree with Parker. This is a

shitty time to decide to be valiant," Fiona said. "If I'm supposed to be tied to your motivation, then remove that question from the equation."

Wyatt didn't have the words to explain this— another feeling he hated. When he interfered before, he'd convinced himself Fiona and Parker would come out on top with the whole Grammie's thing. And they had. It was still a mistake, and this time he couldn't pretend it would do Fiona any good to step forward. "I'll get out of this without you risking your career. How fast do you think the shipping company will drop your contract if they find out about"—*us* sounded presumptuous, as if the three of them were an *us*—"the fucking around and how long it's been going on?"

Fiona pursed her lips until they nearly vanished in the thin line, and a low growl escaped her throat. "But you didn't do this. You're not Tim. Or Devin."

"Devin?" Parker's expression shifted to curiosity.

Wyatt was going to miss the detours these conversations took. "The ex I told you about."

"The reason you went to jail?" Parker asked. "Attractive. Soft-spoken. Flighty? Comes across as a lot more bashful than he really is?"

That was a strangely accurate description. "Yes…"

"I met him in New Orleans. The day of the first bombing, he was in the same bar as me. He told me he worked with you and was a secret, from afar, admirer."

Wyatt's chest squeezed tight.

Parker kept talking. "He was extra interested in

whether or not I knew you and getting me to confess you were sexy."

"Fuck." Wyatt didn't know what to do with the information. Another unknown to add to a rapidly growing list he wanted to tear to shreds and incinerate.

"Was this him?" Fiona asked.

Wyatt shook his head. "The bombs? Not his style, but who the fuck knows? I need to make some phone calls." This was all wrong. Twisted and broken and unraveling.

Fiona stood and squeezed his hand. "We'll go. I'll call Landry and tell him you were with us and we knew it."

"No." Wyatt pulled from her touch and fought the urge to clench his hands into fists.

Fiona raised her brows. "Excuse me? I wasn't asking your permission."

He couldn't let her do this. He would clear his name without muddying hers. Without damaging her career. "I don't want your help." He hid a cringe at the way the words tasted.

"Because you're a big manly man who can take on the world by himself?" Stress leaked into her voice.

"Sure. Why not?" Because this was one thing he could control. He'd let life spiral out of hand everywhere. It was time to start reining things in.

Fiona's scowl etched deep lines in her forehead. "This is my choice."

It should be, but he was going to take it from her. Unlike every other time, he was going to be honest with himself about the reasons. "Why? To bring us closer together? To prove your love?" He didn't know why he used that word, but it worked. He was moving into full-blown asshole mode, if that was what it took to make her back down.

"You're getting a bit ahead of yourself. Or full of yourself. Or something." Parker faltered.

"Am I?" Wyatt pressed forward. "You're both here, aren't you? Dropped everything when I called today. Couldn't wait to think of an excuse to tell me *yes* to coming along on these trips."

"Stop." Fiona spoke through clenched teeth.

Not until he made his point. He'd let his dick lead the way every step when it came to Fiona—wiping out reason, telling him there was more there than really was. "You wanted me to be honest."

"And you're not."

"Just because you don't want to hear it doesn't mean it's untrue." He was about to push her away for good. The gnawing inside hated his decision. He needed to stop listening to his gut and heart. His head kept him in the game. And today, it would do the same for her.

"No," Fiona said. "This is lying through your teeth when you don't need to."

He hated how close she was to creeping inside his thoughts. "This is me, telling you there's no future in what we're doing. Arrest or not. Once your implementation was over, we were going our separate ways. You're a fuck—you and your pretty boyfriend. It was fun, but it was getting old." Wyatt was surprised he didn't gag on the denial.

"Watch it," Parker warned.

Fiona stepped back, toward the door. "You're

full of shit."

Fuck, he hated the hurt in her eyes. That was part of his problem, though. He read so much into her expressions. Wanted a relationship that wasn't meant to be. "Almost always. After all, I fooled you. This is best for everyone. Don't go to Landry. Don't throw your company away for a couple of nights of kinky sex."

She opened her mouth. "I'm not—"

"You are. You know I'm right." He hadn't even convinced himself. How was he supposed to make her believe it? Because he had to. "In fact, let's make this straightforward and end things now. I'll be in court for several weeks"—years—"anyway. You're not going to stick around town for that long. Now's the perfect time for you to go live life. I don't want to play this game anymore."

"You're not serious." It was difficult to tell if Fiona was on the edge of tears or rage. Both, if she felt half of what Wyatt did.

Parker grasped her arm. "He's serious."

"Glad one of you gets it." Wyatt summoned everything he had to keep his voice hard. "Get the fuck out."

Fiona jerked from Parker's grasp and stalked up to Wyatt. She held his gaze, her jaw set in a hard line. She jabbed him in the chest with her finger. "Do you think I'm dumb?" The vehemence in her voice caught him off-guard.

"No."

"Insincere? Unobservant?"

Definitely not. "Your point?"

"Then maybe you feel like I'm inattentive. That

I wasn't an active participant in pretty much any conversation we've ever had, from the first time we met?"

Wyatt needed her out of his head. Both the thought of her and the way she honed in on what he held back. "I was selling you a product—me. Telling you what you needed to hear, in order for me to get what I wanted."

"You didn't mean a single word of it." A storm of fury sparked in her eyes.

He meant every word of it. "Not one."

"Every time you picked my company over sex. When you said you wanted me to know the real you."

"You were a challenge. A tough one. But— achievement unlocked. I need a new game." He had to hurt her, to keep her from coming back.

"Really." Her voice was flat.

He wouldn't crack. Wouldn't think about the fact that this was the most difficult lie he'd ever told. "Really."

Fiona stared him down. Her nostrils flared, and a flush spread across her cheeks and down her neck.

He refused to flinch.

"Fine. Fuck you. We'll do it your way." She spun on her toe and walked from the room.

Parker looked at Wyatt with pity. "Good luck with your life," he said, sounding like he didn't mean a word of it.

Wyatt sank into the desk chair and dropped his face into his hands. Hardest sale he'd ever made, and possibly the one he'd regret longer than any other, but it was over. He'd done what he needed to, pushed them away, and he could get back to things the way they were supposed to be.

He needed clearing his name to be this simple. And possibly hurt less. Because the way his heart was shredded, it wouldn't withstand another round of pain.

Chapter Twenty

Wyatt needed something to focus on besides what he'd just done. If he examined things too closely, none of his actions made sense.

Of course they do. He'd let his life spiral out of control since he met Fiona and Parker. He should have realized his world was out of control without tragedy striking. There were so many points along the way where it should've been obvious. With Ginny. When he pulled strings to trick Fiona into seeing him, all but begging her to come up to his office so he could apologize.

He wasn't that man. He didn't lose his shit for anyone.

There was something to distract him, though. He could thank Parker for that.

Wyatt grabbed his phone and called Devin.

"Hey, handsome." Devin's smooth greeting was like salt in open wounds.

Wyatt didn't have to pretend here. There was no reason to wear a mask. "Why were you in New

Orleans?"

"What makes you think I was?"

"A friend told me."

Devin clucked. "A *friend*. Sexy guy with a camera, who radiates charisma? He's *so* not your type. He told me he didn't know you."

Wyatt wasn't playing games. "Why were you in New Orleans?"

"For business, just like you."

"That's convenient." Wyatt let his sneer slide into his tone.

"No more convenient than you being there and in Atlanta and in Philadelphia—should I go on?—at the same time as Fiona Walters."

Wyatt drove a fist toward the desk, stopping short of striking the surface. He needed his rage to stay cold. If he couldn't get a direct answer to one question, he'd move to the next. "Are you behind these bombings?"

Devin's gasp was the embodiment of scandalized. "I could never. Why would you think such horrible things about me?"

"Experience?"

"You see, this is why we didn't work out. You think so poorly of me."

Wyatt tried to push down the fury that boiled inside, but he was losing the fight. "We didn't work out, because you stalked and assaulted several women."

"I didn't do anything you haven't."

The comment should have rolled off Wyatt, but it wormed under his skin instead. "Why. Were you. In New Orleans?"

"I'm trying to get you fired." It sounded like the most honest thing Devin had said to him… possibly ever. "Turns out, you took care of that yourself. Blowing up packages? That's beneath you."

"You think I did this?"

"They arrested you."

Wyatt was surprised he had the restraint to not throw his phone across the room. "I was set up."

"Hmm… That excuse worked for you last time. You think it'll pan out again?" Devin asked. "I have to run. Ciao, lover."

Wyatt tossed his phone at the bed, before he could fling it at the nearest wall. He shouldn't let the conversation get to him. Instead, he should be on the phone with Charles and ask what it would take to get Landry to look at Devin as a suspect.

Out of the entire conversation, the parts focused on Fiona stuck in his head. *I didn't do anything you haven't.* The taunt was in Devin's voice.

It wasn't true, on the surface, but Wyatt had sure as fuck blurred some of the lines of consent by withholding information.

It didn't matter. Fiona had been shown the reality now, and she was gone. It was better for everyone this way.

Wyatt needed to put her out of his mind and call his lawyer.

♥♥♥

Fiona desperately wanted to learn whatever trick Wyatt was using to slather on the *I don't give a fuck*, because her insides felt like they'd been cut to ribbons. She was grateful to Parker, who let her squeeze the life from his hand as they walked back to their room. They'd move to a different motel tomorrow. Probably one out of state. There was no reason to stay here.

It was a dumb idea to take Wyatt's call, to begin with. Stupid to stay in the same place. Again.

Parker unlocked the door and let them in. Part of her wanted him to say something. To give her a chance to lash out.

But she wouldn't. Not at Parker. He was her pillar, anchoring her in the storm of bad, wrong, boneheaded decisions.

"Hey." He placed a finger under her chin and raised her head, so he could look her in the eye. He brushed his lips over hers, and warmth mingled with the internal wounds. It didn't heal anything, but it lessened the sting. "No regrets."

She laughed in spite of herself, and a few tears broke free and slid down her cheeks. "I don't... I can't..." Her thoughts were so jumbled, she couldn't put them into words.

Parker slid his hand to the back of her neck and kissed her on the forehead, before pressing his head to hers. "I know what you're thinking."

"How?" She sure as hell didn't.

"I know *you*. So much better than I thought possible, after the last couple of months. And I'm grateful for that." He trailed his fingers down her arm, to grasp her hand and tug her to sit next to him on the bed. "You've got this mental war going on. The half of you wondering how you could have missed all the signs, not once but twice. How could you have kept falling down that hole with Wyatt, given your past with him? And the other half of you insists you weren't wrong this time."

That sounded about right. She leaned into Parker and pulled his arm around her waist. "Either way, he lied again. Whether it was his words today or those leading up to it. How do you still love me?" She nearly choked on the question.

"Because I do."

It should have been the perfect answer, but it made her feel worse. "I've spent the entire length of our romantic relationship bouncing back and forth over how I feel about another man. And you've stood by me."

"And you'd do the same for me." Parker spoke with conviction.

Would she? "I would. As long as we were still together at the end of the day." They'd danced around the subject before, even said some of the same words, but today they sank in with a solidness she couldn't deny.

"Also, the asshole is lying about how he feels." Parker kissed the top of her head. "Not that it's your right or mine to change his words if he's set on sticking to them."

This time her smile didn't hurt so much. "Where are we going tomorrow?"

"I thought we'd rent a car and drive west. See what we can find hidden on the back roads and highways."

She liked that idea.

"What are you going to do about Wyatt?" he asked.

"Give him what he asked for—demanded—

space wise. If he wants to go back to being a grumpy old bachelor, fine with me." It wasn't. But her head wasn't on straight to examine alternatives. "And I'm calling Landry."

"Nick is going to be furious."

Not what she wanted to hear, but a fair point. She was fifty-fifty, when it came to pushing away or keeping the men in her life. Why not add her brother to the list and tip the scales? "I should probably warn him."

"Do you want me to stick around, as moral support, or do you want your privacy?"

She wanted the support, but she was concerned that, if things broke down into shouting with Nick, Parker would step in on her behalf. She liked the thought, but this was her battle to fight. "Only one of us needs to be pissed off. Do you want to go get some filming in?"

"Sure. It hardly seems important, but I should."

Gratitude and love swelled inside. She threw her arms around his neck and buried her face in his shoulder. "I won't make you regret sticking with me."

"I know. I trust you." He squeezed her tight, before letting her go. "I'll get out of your way. Good luck with Nick."

Fiona waited while Parker tugged on a baseball cap, meant to hide his face from the casual person looking for him, and grabbed his gear. She fidgeted with her phone until he was gone.

It took her several minutes to gather her courage, before she dialed her brother.

The moment he answered, she blurted out, "We

need to talk."

So much for easing into this.

"All right… Are you okay?" Nick asked.

"No. I'm fine in the ways you're probably thinking, but… you're going to be furious. I ask that you hold the shouting until I finish."

"That sounds bad. This is about Wyatt?"

"Yes." Fiona told him everything except the intimate details, including things they'd already covered. She didn't want to leave out any important notes. She dove into how she and Parker met Wyatt. His offer to act as a tour guide for Parker, before they had any idea who he worked for. Their giving him a second chance, after they did know. That she thought she might be in love with two men, despite it being a bad idea.

She expected a reaction at some point. A snort or something. Even the *love* revelation didn't draw a squeak from Nick.

Fantastic. He'd crossed into too-furious-to-speak territory.

"Is there more?" he asked.

"Isn't that enough?"

His barking laugh made her cringe. "Why are you telling me all of this? Did I do something to piss you off, and I didn't realize it?"

"Because Wyatt isn't the bomber." Not *quite* the right answer, but she needed a new wave of strength.

"And Ms. Passion wouldn't have anything to pin on *you* if you weren't following this asshole around."

Fiona's emotions were too raw for her to ignore

the surge of rage. "I went where the jobs took me. Are you going to tell me next that it's my fault Tim did what he did?'

"*No*. I'm—" His sigh hurt her eardrums. "This isn't about the sex. It's not about your personal life. I've got opinions about what you and Parker are doing, but if you want to fuck up your relationship, feel free—"

"But that's not what this is about." She let the sarcasm drip from her voice.

"It's not. It's about what it does to us. You fucked a client. Before? You didn't know. Afterward? What the fuck were you doing?"

"I'm sorry it came to this." She couldn't apologize for the rest of it. "But he's not guilty, and regardless of what you think about Wyatt and me— even if you're such an asshole you don't care what happens to an innocent man—if he's in jail, they're not looking for the real bomber."

"If you destroy the company we've built, because you wanted to fuck around…"

Fiona didn't know what Nick could threaten her with that was worse than the current circumstance. "Then what?"

"I don't know. I trust you, but I don't understand this. Any of what you were thinking. This man lied to you. He tried to break you. He fucked you over in more ways than one."

Each word hammered another nail of reality in. What *had* she been thinking? "None of that means he deserves to go to jail."

"I hate to be the one to say this—or rather, I'm surprised no one else has—but after you found out who he was, you knew what you were walking into."

"I really didn't." Because she'd pretended she could extract her heart from this mess. That all she wanted was another tumble or two, to get him out of her system. She should have seen her obsession. Why had she been so blind?

Another sigh, but this one quieter. It sank into her soul. "Call a lawyer of your own before you do this," Nick said. "I'll stand by you publicly, but I don't know if I can forgive you if you destroy what we built."

"I understand."

As she hung up, the conversation bounced in her head, mingling with Parker's and Wyatt's voices. It turned out Nick did tip the scales. He was right. When she set out to do this with Parker, the one hesitation she had was that acting irresponsibly—impulsively—would hurt her and Nick's company.

Instead of keeping that in mind, she let lust drive her. That hot, intense sensation she felt whenever Wyatt was around. Worse, she'd convinced herself it meant more than that.

Maybe it could have become real, maybe not, but it wasn't now. She never should have let something so fleeting spill out into the rest of her life.

What have I done?

Chapter Twenty-One

Parker wasn't talking to the camera as he walked. He'd be pressed to meet the livestreaming portion of his requirements for the week, but the frame of mind he was in, he'd make a lousy tour guide.

He was barely aware of what he was filming. The conversation—fight?—with Wyatt looped in his head. He knew what was going on, because he'd do the same thing in Wyatt's place. He'd try like hell to not take anyone down with him.

Wyatt may want them to believe he was more selfish than that, but Parker didn't buy it.

Why not? What did Wyatt do to raise himself above the sabotaging asshole they originally met?

It wasn't any one thing. It was the culmination of his behavior.

Not that it mattered. That chapter of Parker and Fiona's life was closed. They had a solid relationship, and this would hurt her for a while, but it wouldn't pull them apart.

He tried to focus on filming. The city held so much beauty and vibrancy, it was easy to capture and hard to contain.

His phone rang. He paused the camera and stepped aside, to answer the call from Chloe. "This is Parker." He wouldn't be rude, but he wasn't feeling the friendliness either.

"This is Chloe with Rinslet Media. Do you have a few minutes?" Her cool tone matched his.

"Sure."

"We're prepping our next competition round, but no surprises this time. Not for the content creators. We need to do some damage control around the incident—"

"That's really what you're calling it?" Parker couldn't hide his irritation.

Chloe's silence was deafening.

She finally spoke. "That's what we're calling it. And while we're on the subject of Ms. Passion, if you ever make demands of me again—"

"What?" Parker's patience was thinner than he realized. "You had the power and contacts to do what needed to be done. I don't have any regrets."

"I don't have to keep you in this contest." Chloe's frustration pushed aside her professionalism.

"You could eject me, if I'm that big a problem." Parker expected a sick feeling at the words. He should be praying she wouldn't call his bluff. But was he actually bluffing?

She *tsk*ed a couple of times. "I understand why you did what you did when the situation came up. I'm asking for professional courtesy right now."

That was fair. "Competition round?"

"What you did with Jeremy—you on camera, his performance, hitting both your subscribers—was a big hit. What are the odds you'll be in Chicago any time soon?"

Parker didn't know what one had to do with the other. "I haven't picked my next destination." *Let's drive west* wasn't much of a plan. Chloe's words clicked together. "You have the chefs in Chicago. Julie and the TV guy?"

"Dante. That's them. Any interest in filming a cooking show?"

"Could be fun." As long as they weren't making hand-crafted candy.

"I'm glad you think that." A hint of amusement leaked into her voice. "This will be a two-part act. You stream their show—which they rarely do live—to yours and their channel. After, they have a friend who will show you around the city. You keep filming. As in, you put in the hour for them and don't turn off the camera for the next three after that."

A three-hour tour. The Gilligan's Island theme song bounced in his thoughts, both taunting him and making him smile. "That's a long show."

"I've seen you when you're in the groove. You'll rock this. When can you be there?"

"Two or three days."

"Great." She sounded sincere. "We're planning this for a week-ish from now. I'll send you the final times before the public announcement, in case you want to be someplace else until that day."

Getting out of town would be good. Taking Fiona away from all of this. Parker didn't even care about the change of scenery for himself this time; she needed a break. "Sounds like a plan. Anything else?"

"Yeah..." Chloe dragged out the word.

He waited for her to finish the thought. And waited. "Which is?"

"Regarding Ms. Passion. Any idea why she'd do this to Fiona? Why she'd risk her channel, to say those things?"

Insanity didn't know reason? "I wanted to ask you the same question."

"I wish I knew. I met her the same way I interviewed all of you, before this started. She's not unhinged. Or she is, and I missed it. Or she jumped off the deep end since. But there's no hint of this at all in her work. She's been doing the sex-toy reviews for years and knows exactly where that line is between obscene and not, to keep her channel from being tagged as *Adult*. I can't fathom why she'd destroy all of that, for no reason."

"It's not as though she was going to get away with it." Parker had gone over similar questions and not reached a conclusion. But he didn't know the woman. An online persona was easy to use as a mask. "She had to know the least you'd to do her was kick her out." And in this case, YouTube had deleted her account.

"So no one has an answer."

"Ms. Passion does. Maybe someday she'll share it." He raked his fingers through his hair. "This is stressful for everyone. I get it. I'm sorry for what you're dealing with."

Chloe's laugh was dry. "I've dealt with worse. Google it."

Parker wasn't sure he wanted to know.

"But I'll give you this much," Chloe said. "You've helped uncover more holes in our concept in the last couple of months than we expected to find the entire first year. I should be thanking you."

It was a shitty thing to be known for. "Don't mention it. Please."

"Fair enough. Stay safe and enjoy Chicago."

"Thanks." Parker disconnected.

This was what he and Fiona needed. The road trip he suggested. A couple of days off. A new place.

He couldn't ignore the gnawing inside that insisted this wasn't the easy escape he hoped for. Worse, his looming dread didn't have to do with Fiona's attraction to Wyatt. It was tied to something he hadn't seen yet, and the last thing he was going to do was challenge the universe by asking, *What now?*

Chapter Twenty-Two

Fiona watched Parker's competition round from the anonymity of a hotel room on the other side of downtown Chicago. She'd rather be with him, but neither one of them relished the idea of her trying to stay out of the camera's way for his city tour.

She'd take this a hundred times over her life a week ago—the mess that culminated with her telling Landry that she was Wyatt's alibi.

Landry asked her in every way imaginable why she'd kept the information to herself for so long.

Her answer was the same each time—she didn't believe the information was any more relevant than giving him details about her sex life, but when she realized why they were asking, she was happy to make sure Wyatt was clear.

Landry didn't look like he believed her, but her lawyer cut the conversation short when it got repetitive, and Fiona walked away.

On her laptop screen, Parker wrapped things up in the kitchen. He kept up the chatter with Julie and

Dante, while the pair cleaned up. The couple was adorable on camera. They radiated chemistry, and each touch—no matter how small—came with a smile. Fiona hoped to meet them when the cameras weren't on.

The drive up here had been nice. The scenery was stunning. There were so many trees, some shifting toward fall colors, while others were still green. Chicago was amazing, the skyline rising up in architectural spikes against a flat horizon.

Parker wasn't on screen much, but she could tell from his voice that he was having fun.

She flopped back on the hotel bed and listened for a while. To Parker chatting. To Christopher joining the conversation. To the train ride further into the city.

It wasn't as much fun as seeing the action. If she couldn't be there with them, at least she could watch. She sat up again and focused on the screen.

Fiona only had to watch for a few minutes, to see that Christopher was as close to Julie and Dante as they were with each other. The three of them made a cute triad. Fiona couldn't imagine Parker and Wyatt swapping the type of subtle but intimate touches the men did on screen.

She shouldn't be imagining Wyatt at all. He'd made his decision, and she needed to get him out of her head. Doing so would help with the pit that formed in her stomach every time she thought his name.

Trying to convince herself last time that he was gone didn't work so well, and they weren't this close. Why did she think she could forget him this time?

What were the odds he'd take her call? Could she go through that kind of heartache again?

No. She had more respect for herself than that, and she loved Parker too much, to make him put up with it.

If Wyatt wanted in—was willing to admit he felt something more than *I need to get off*—the three of them could make things work.

He'd made it clear he wasn't interested. That was that.

Fiona tried to lose herself in the guided tour of Chicago. Christopher was good at what he did. He pointed out several places Parker could check out later. Everyone was laughing and having fun.

A pounding on the hotel door made Fiona's heart leap into her throat.

"Fiona Walters? FBI." The booming voice carried into the room.

Acid surged up her esophagus. She swallowed it down. Any other thought evaporated. She walked on shaky legs to the door and peered through the peephole. "Show me your badge."

There were four men in the hallway, stretched in a weird fish-eye view. The one nearest her held up a badge.

That didn't help. She couldn't identify it, even without the distortion.

The hotel desk clerk stepped forward. She did recognize *him*. "These men are who they say they are. I'll vouch for them," he said.

That didn't calm her hammering heart. She opened the door. "Is something wrong?" It might be a dim question, but she didn't know what else to ask.

"I'm Agent Spike. I'm here to take you into custody."

"Why?" Her pulse pounded in her ears so loudly, she was surprised she heard him. "I want a lawyer."

"It's protective custody." Agent Spike's voice softened, and so did his expression.

"Why?" she asked again.

"There's been another bombing."

Oh fuck. She was going to be sick. "Where?"

"A few blocks away. The package exploded in the night drop box."

Jesus. Fiona's world tilted and spun, until she swore she was going to pass out.

♥♥♥

The only thing Parker would change about tonight would be not having Fiona here. And maybe the tour guide. Christopher was nice enough, but he wasn't Wyatt.

Parker's phone rang with the familiar tune he'd assigned to Fiona. "Hold on," he said. "I wouldn't take this, but she wouldn't call if it wasn't important."

"No worries." Dante came to a stop a few feet away. Julie and Christopher paused too.

Parker kept his camera arm extended, focused on them. "Keep talking. I'm still rolling." He pressed his phone to his ear. "What's up?" He was quiet. The camera mic should filter him out as background noise.

"There was another bomb." Fiona sounded on the verge of panic. "The FBI have me in *protective* custody. Call Nick, please, and meet me at the police station."

"Whoa." He wished he'd heard her wrong. "Red, slow down. Tell me more."

"I'm still finding out for myself. I need you here. Please?" Her terror bled across the line.

"Okay. I'll be there. Give me an address."

She did, and he tapped it into his phone, then read it back to her twice, to make sure he had it right. "I'll be there as quickly as I can." He hung up.

"Is everything all right?" Julie watched him with concern.

"No. It's really not." He shoved the camera at Christopher. "I'll pick this up from you later. I need to go." Parker didn't care that they were live or that he'd just handed a thousand-dollar piece of equipment to a near stranger. Fiona was the only thing that mattered. "Can you tell me the fastest way to get to this address?" He showed Christopher the phone, off screen.

"Hail a cab. It's only a few miles away."

"Thank you. Sorry to cut and run."

"It's fine. Whatever it is, go." Dante was kind.

Parker was already turning toward the street.

♥ ♥ ♥

Wyatt sat in his hotel room, watching as Parker was shown around Chicago by a sickeningly sweet trio of friends—lovers, probably. This was a foolish way to spend his time.

Not that he could come up with anything better to do. Job hunting was on hold. He'd watched everything on TV. Parker was entertaining. Always.

The camera angle shifted, and Parker's voice grew distant. Muffled but worried.

Curiosity and concern filled Wyatt.

A moment later, the camera tilted toward the ground, and Parker said, "No, it's really not. I'll pick this up from you later. I need to go."

More snippets of conversation were exchanged, most of them bleeding into the surrounding noise of the city, and then the camera moved back to Dante and Julie. But the narrator's voice was Christopher's.

What the fuck was this?

Wyatt's hotel room door slammed against the wall loud enough it sounded like a gunshot.

"Get down on the floor. *Now.*" Agent Landry pointed a gun at Wyatt's forehead.

No. This was too familiar. The adrenaline racing through Wyatt's veins dried his mouth. He flattened himself on the ground, hands out to his sides.

"Slowly, shift to your knees and put your hands behind your head," Landry shouted.

If there was ever a time not to protest, this was it. Wyatt followed each command to the syllable. He didn't complain when another agent jerked his arms behind his back and cuffed him. There was no joke to be made here, about them buying him dinner first.

"Wyatt Lindberg, you've violated the terms of your bond. You have the right to remain silent."

Wyatt tuned out the rest. He kept the grunts to a minimal when they yanked him to his feet. He suspected he would have been half-dragged to one of the cars waiting in front of the hotel if he weren't taller than the officer leading him.

People were out on the sidewalk and peering through their windows, several of them with cameras out.

Fantastic.

They shoved him in the back of the car and peeled onto the road. His arms were twisted at an awkward angle, and his neck ached, but there weren't a lot of comfortable positions when he was cuffed like this.

"What's this about?" Wyatt finally asked when he was mostly sure no one was going to shoot him.

Landry glanced back from his spot in the passenger seat. "You wanted your lawyer so desperately last time. I suggest you have him on hand again, before you and I exchange any other words."

Wyatt's gut threatened to cave in on itself.

Chapter Twenty-Three

Fiona sobbed with relief when they let Parker join her in the questioning room Agent Spike asked her to wait in.

She sprinted the few feet to greet Parker and hugged him tight. He squeezed back, and the embrace helped put her back together.

"I'm sorry for interrupting your stream." Her words were muffled by his chest.

He rested his forehead on the top of her head. "It doesn't matter. Are you all right?"

"I'm better than I was five minutes ago."

Parker led her back to the seat she'd vacated, took her spot, and pulled her into his lap. "Tell me what's going on."

Right. That was the least she could offer. "There was another bomb, near the hotel. They told me I'm not being charged. That this is *protective custody*. I asked if it was proof that they shouldn't have arrested Wyatt. Apparently, since he was out on bond, it's not proof of anything. They do think he's got an accomplice who's local, though."

"Why did they pick you up?" The absentminded stroke of his thumb along the inside of her wrist was comforting.

"Because I'm the common thread in all of this, according to them. My business card, the photos of me on the phone, and that every explosion happened in a city I was in."

"Well, *fuck*." Parker's breath was warm against her skin. "I called Nick. He'll have an attorney here soon."

She curled into him as much as was possible in the metal chair. "Thank you. Again."

"What do you think of Chicago so far?" he asked, teasing mingling with his stress.

"The hospitality leaves a bit to be desired. I'm wishing I had a frequent-visit punch-card for police stations."

His laugh rumbled through her, calming her nerves further.

They sat in silence, but it was different than being in the room alone. This was comfortable and right.

"Did you ask? Did they tell you?" Parker's questions came out of nowhere.

Fiona didn't need clarification. "I think they were trying to comfort me. Or threaten me. It's difficult to tell with Agent Spike. Wyatt's back in custody. They picked him up about the same time as me."

"Not that you care?"

Her chuckle was bitter. "So much more than is healthy." She was certain their conversation was being monitored. It didn't matter. She'd already told the FBI enough about her relationship with Wyatt that none of this would be a surprise or damning.

The silence settled in again. She didn't know how much time passed. Ten minutes? Thirty? It was probably only two or three. The door clanged open, and Agent Spike walked in with a man wearing a polo shirt and khakis.

"Fiona Walters?" Mr. Business Casual extended his hand. He had a faint French accent. "I'm Michele Cambuse. Your brother Nick has retained me to represent you."

She extracted herself from Parker's lap, to shake Michele's hand. "Thank you for coming."

"Of course. Now"—Michele turned to Agent Spike—"why is my client still in custody? Is she being charged?"

"No. But we need to discuss the terms of her release."

"There are no terms. You can't hold her indefinitely. We're going home."

Spike stepped between Michele and the door. "This is for your client's safety. We need her someplace we can have an agent watching her at all times."

Fiona didn't like the sound of that. It felt so… Big Brother.

"Ridiculous," Michele spat. "I read the highlights of the case. She hasn't been in the vicinity of any of the explosions. What good does that do?"

"She's the only link we have, and we'd hate for the next bomb to be the one that reaches her, if she's the target."

"It's all right. An agent watching me is no big deal." Fiona wanted to go home. Or back to the hotel. Someplace that wasn't here.

Spike looked at Parker. "You're the boyfriend? The one shooting all the video?"

"That's me."

"We have another request. We'd like copies of all of the footage you've shot since you met Wyatt Lindberg. And we'd like a look at your cameras, as well."

Parker snorted. "That's my livelihood. Literally. You can't take it away."

"You can surrender everything now, and we'll turn the hardware around as quickly as possible, or I can get a warrant, and the devices may sit in an evidence locker for months."

Fiona felt like Agent Spike was enjoying this a little too much.

Parker nodded. "I'll bring it all by tomorrow."

"He wants receipts for everything," Michele said. "And if any of it comes back with even a scratch, you'll replace it."

"Bullshit." Agent Spike rolled his eyes.

Michele shrugged. "They're doing you a favor. You could try to get a warrant…"

"Fine." Spike stepped aside and opened the door. "You're free to go. A local officer will see you back to your hotel, to gather your things, and we'll relocate you."

Fiona wasn't going to argue. She had a suspicion she needed to save her strength to fight more important battles. This wouldn't be the last one.

They were driven to their hotel in the back of a

squad car. It smelled like soap, mixed with vomit. Fiona didn't know if she was grateful or not that she hadn't eaten in several hours.

The officer said he'd be waiting outside the door. At least they had a little privacy.

The moment they were in the room, Fiona called her brother. She set the phone on the table and put it on speaker, so she could work while she talked.

"Hey, Red." Nick's tired voice was hollow, coming from the tiny device. "Parker was sparse with details. What's going on?"

Fiona filled him in on the custody, the bombing, everything she knew, and thanked him for sending a competent lawyer to watch over her.

"You're welcome." Nick sounded like his soul had been beaten down.

Fiona frowned. "What's going on? What aren't you telling me?"

"We can talk about it later. You've got a lot to worry about."

That didn't sound right. "I'm in a holding pattern. Tell me. Why do you sound as though you've been tugged through the wringer?"

"Your connection with Wyatt was leaked to the media. The shipping company knows about your *affair*. They've canceled our contract."

I'm sorry felt like a weak comeback. Then again, so did, *We knew it was coming.* "What can I do?"

"Nothing. Please, don't do anything."

The request cut her to the bone. "Nick?"

"They're threatening legal action. For non-disclosure. Breach of contract. If they make good on even a tiny portion of what they mentioned, we won't survive financially."

Wyatt didn't have the luxury of being processed into holding this time. He was booked, stripped of his belongings, and given a stunning orange jumpsuit.

He was seated in a questioning room and told his attorney was on the way. Landry refused to give him more information.

Wyatt didn't know how long he'd been waiting, but the numbness in his ass and the number of times the Jeopardy theme had repeated in his head indicated it was *a while*.

It was even longer before the door finally creaked open and Charles joined him.

The lawyer sat across from him. "I'll tell you everything I've been given, and then my advice is to stop protecting this woman and spill everything you know."

Wyatt growled at the term *this woman*.

Chuck rolled his eyes. "She already told them she was with you. If your story matches hers, it will be a lot easier."

"What did she tell them?" Wyatt should be more focused on his situation, but if Fiona had talked to someone and he was still here, he was fucked either way. He loathed the idea of taking her down with him.

Who was he becoming?

"You'd better hope you know what she said, at least to an extent." Charles's tone was matter of fact. "Because it's the best chance you have to get out of here.”

“Fine. Tell them I’ll talk about all of it. Stop me if I get too damning.”

Charles strode to the door and hammered on it until agent Landry opened it.

“We’re ready,” Charles said.

He and Landry returned to the table. This time Charles sat next to Wyatt.

Landry set a digital recorder between them. “The camera is also on. This is to ensure there’s no misunderstanding.”

“Fine.” Wyatt preferred that, anyway. He didn’t trust this man to not twist his words. Landry reminded him too much of himself. “Do you have questions, or do you just want me to start rambling?”

“Tell me about the afternoon at the winery, and I’ll stop you if I need details.”

Wyatt did. He left out the part about asking Fiona to leave the panties at home and what happened after. He did disclose that, at the time, she had no idea who he worked for.

“But you knew who she was.” Landry had an odd habit. He’d trace his finger along the edge of the recorder without making contact.

“She and her boyfriend are minor internet celebrities, and his shtick was based on her job. Everyone watching knew.”

“Why didn’t you tell her who you were?” Landry’s expression never shifted, but he wiggled his fingers.

Son of a bitch had a tell, and he thought he was getting what he wanted from Wyatt. Too bad that wasn’t good news. “I was trying to win the same contract she was, and I didn't want her to know."

"So you were actively trying to destroy her career."

Wyatt cringed at the phrasing. He'd worked so hard to convince himself his actions would do the opposite in the long run. But it was denial then. "No."

Landry raised his brows. Another break in the facade. *Interesting.*

"I didn't care about her job. It was all about mine."

Landry clenched his hands, but his fingers still twitched. "Why didn't you tell me any of this before?"

"Because it could ruin her career." *Wow*, that sounded weak. Next he'd be saying, *but I've changed.*

"It could keep you out of prison."

That was the wrong approach for Landry to take. "Apparently not," Wyatt said.

"I'm not understanding this. You know she has a boyfriend, right? Not that that means much to some people, but I've seen them together."

So had Wyatt, and he wasn't going to argue the intricacies of their relationship with this man. Fiona loved him as much as she did Parker. It should have been an egotistical thought, but it hurt instead.

Because Wyatt felt the same. This was a real shitty time for personal revelation. Especially if it required admitting he might not have a chance to make things right. In an attempt to exercise control, he'd surrendered the one bit of it he had left.

His entire thought process took a heartbeat, and he wasn't going to share any of it with Landry. Case details, sure. His fucked-up heart? No. "I figured my innocence would win out," Wyatt said. "No reason to slander her if I wasn't going down."

Landry snorted. "Wow. You almost made me believe that *innocence* line. Who's your accomplice?"

"I'm sorry—what?" Wyatt would have feigned ignorance anyway, but he had no idea what Landry was talking about.

"The bomb in Chicago. You were here the whole time. Who helped you plant it? Did they know? Did you trick them into it, the same way you tricked Ms. Walters into keeping you company before she knew who you were?"

"I didn't have anything to do with the bombs." Wyatt needed to get into this guy's head. Figure out what approach it would take to sell him. Wyatt could convince anyone of anything. The truth shouldn't be such a difficult pitch.

Landry stood. "I was under the impression you were going to tell me everything."

"I've told you everything you've asked. You want more details about the time I spent with Fiona? I'll give you those. You want my travel schedule for the last couple of months? Every stop I've made? Every appointment I had? I'll give you that. But I can't tell you what I don't know."

"That's okay." Landry turned toward the door. "You can stay here and keep us company until your arraignment."

If they thought a couple of days in jail were going to break him into admitting something he didn't do, they were stupid. But if his only choice was to cool his heels, he'd do it.

An officer put Wyatt back in his cell. It turned out not having anything to do for hours on end was a dangerous way for a mind to pass the time. The first day or so, he looped through everything he knew about his arrest, searching for clues he'd missed. Ways to prove his innocence. Indicators of who'd framed him.

He kept coming back to Devin. He'd given his ex's name to Charles and Landry.

Devin had alibis that were apparently better than Wyatt's. How that was possible, Wyatt had no idea.

When the string of circular thoughts ran its course more times than he could count, his mind fell back to Fiona. The one place he both hated going and wanted to stay at.

Was she all right? They thought she was the target, for whatever reason. Was Parker doing okay? At least they were taking care of each other…

It was an odd perspective to take, and when his mind veered in that direction, he had no choice but to follow. He'd spent so much time telling Parker how lucky he was. It was meant to be lip service, but Wyatt meant it.

Fiona was lucky too. Wyatt had replayed that last live stream in his head enough that he knew it was her, calling and that Parker had dropped everything without hesitating, to be what she needed.

Wyatt had shoved them both out the door under the flimsy excuses of *protecting them* and *staying in control*.

He was such a fucking idiot.

What would it be like, to be part of what Fiona and Parker had? Each time the question made an appearance in the rotation, he latched onto it harder, asking, *Why can't I?*

Because he might have fucked up that chance. Did he want to be a part of it?

Damn straight, he did.

The last time he saw them, she didn't believe anything he said to push her away. Neither did Parker. But Wyatt pushed anyway. Did he break his chances?

No. He wouldn't believe that. If he made it out of here, he'd find them. He'd drop the masks. He'd ask—beg—for a second chance.

If he made it out of here.

Chapter Twenty-Four

Six months ago, this was Fiona's life. Work for eight hours. Go home. Watch TV and online videos. Eat. Sleep.

There was none of what back-then-her would have called *irresponsible behavior*. Now-her had learned to enjoy—even crave—the different city every few days, the new samples of culture, and the sex with two incredible men.

Okay, so her old self might have a point about that last one being irresponsible. All of Nick's emails were terse and business only. He didn't reply to any personal questions. Even to, *How are you?*

Parker sat next to her on the couch, where she was working, and kissed her on the cheek. "How's the deadline coming?"

"It's not." Who was she, anymore? He was the one thing she didn't have any doubts about, in this whole big mess.

He couldn't even go out and shoot video, because the FBI had all his camera equipment. The only not-tragic thing about that was that he didn't turn over any of the X-rated footage he had of Fiona. He never kept that with his other videos, and he'd decided there was no reason to even mention the clips existed, unless the Feds had a warrant for *everything*.

Not that he'd have a long leash anyway. He and Fiona were watched even when they went down to the lobby for an afternoon sugar fix from the gift shop.

All of their food was delivered, and the drivers had to drop it at a nearby room, where the agent on duty would bring it over.

"What are you up to?" Fiona asked.

He'd offered to give her space, to work, but apparently that wasn't happening for either of them. "I was browsing exotic locales to visit. Thinking I've still never made it to Red Square in the spring. Wondering if I could get a Russian visa and what the odds were I could broadcast from there."

Better than of them walking out of here before Wyatt's arraignment without a human shadow. "I'm in. How do we make it happen?" she said.

"Is your work saved?"

Fiona nodded.

Parker took her laptop and switched to a browser window. He opened YouTube and frowned. "You've got a unique browsing history."

It wasn't odd, though, as far as she was concerned. The countless nights, filled with dreams of Tim coming for her again, were the perfect reason to watch as many videos of his legal proceedings as she could.

"I'm sad that he succeeded." Parker's comment was soft.

"In what?"

"Making sure you never forget him."

Right. Another thing Fiona hated—living in fear, even before the bombings, always looking over her shoulder.

Something caught her eye in one of the thumbnails, as Parker hit *Search*.

"Stop. Go back." She reached over him and clicked to return to the previous screen. "It can't be." She was tired. Her mind was playing tricks. She was going stir crazy. The clip was gone, though.

She grabbed her computer back. "Where is it?"

"Red?"

She didn't dare say, because it couldn't be real. She would have seen it before now. What was the scene? The courthouse before Tim's arraignment. In the crowds. She typed in a search phrase and scanned thumbnails.

None of them were right. She typed another one.

"Fiona? Talk to me."

"Yeah. It's fine. Hang on." She flew threw five more combinations of words, and none of them produced the right results.

Fiona is a liar. The phrase flowed through her fingers before her mind registered the meaning. She'd been so tired the last time she typed that. The day Wyatt was arrested. When Ms. Passion made her last competition video.

The browser whirred, and results were returned. Her heart dropped into her stomach. She didn't even need to hit *Play*. There it was, right in front of her. She set the image to full screen and pointed.

Parker leaned over her shoulder. "No shit."

It was the guy who had picked a fight with Parker in Atlanta. He stood on the courthouse steps, at the fringes of the handful of media, as Tim was led inside.

"Coincidence?" Half of Fiona wanted it to be, and the other half needed this to mean something.

Parker shook his head. "Nothing about this has been coincidence. Are there more shots of him? Maybe from other days?"

Fiona would have noticed them.

That wasn't true. She was focused on Tim, not background players. "I don't know."

They spent the next couple of hours poring through every video they could find around Tim's trial. Not that there was a lot of footage from the actual event. The only people who cared about it, outside of family, were the vloggers and their followers, who were either pro- or anti-Fiona.

But that meant there were a lot of clips of people talking to neighbors. Photos collected from yearbooks, social media, and anyplace that might allow the video maker to claim *Exclusive*.

So many of them were young Tim. No one else.

There was one someone had supposedly stripped from an old cached version of a webpage. A wedding photo.

"Was he married?" Parker asked.

Not as far as Fiona knew. Not that it would have made a difference in his actions. But it was one of those pieces of information people dug into. "He's next to the groom." She squinted.

"Holy shit." Parker squeezed her knee. "That's him, isn't it?"

The groom was the guy from Atlanta. And the bride looked familiar too. "If she was blonde instead of brunette…"

Parker leaned in to study the screen, his head next to Fiona's. "Ms. Passion," he said.

"Caption says Mr. and Mrs. Gregory and Maxine Simmons. He's Tim's brother."

"Which makes Ms. Passion—Maxine—his sister in law. How did no one notice this?"

Fiona didn't know. "The video only has ten views. Start-up channel, trying to get in on the keywords and missing their mark?"

"I suppose. Wow."

Fiona didn't have any better words for it than that. So many possibilities, almost all of them pointing back to why Ms. Passion had a personal grudge against her.

"Do you think she accused me of the bombing because of this?" It was a reasonable next step in the logic, except that there were pieces missing.

Parker sighed. "She had a vendetta. But she also surrendered a multi-million subscriber channel to come after you. That's willingly throwing away a six-figure income, to twist the knife."

There was still a piece of the puzzle missing, but Fiona couldn't figure out what it was. A tiny voice in the back of her head screamed that Ms. Passion and her husband were behind the bombings.

That made even less sense than accusing Fiona of being responsible. That would mean they'd framed Wyatt. If they knew about him, it would have been a lot easier to expose the affair with Fiona, than blow up several packages and possibly people.

Especially since Fiona was inconvenienced right now, but not in jail.

"Is your brain going nuts with conspiracy theories too?" Parker asked.

"Absolutely insane. But it doesn't matter; they're all so implausible, they don't make sense."

"Nothing about this does," Parker said.

"What if the bombs really are just a coincidence? You and I can't be the only people who were in all three of those cities when the explosions happened."

"Wyatt was in two. Devin was in at least one." Parker scrubbed his face. "Why does it feel like the answer is right there?"

If Fiona knew that, maybe they wouldn't be stuck in a hotel room, with the FBI watching half their moves and one of the men she loved sitting in a jail cell for someone else's crime.

Love. She should recoil from the thought. Reprimand herself for being naive about Wyatt. Like she'd been doing for weeks.

She was tired of lying to herself, though. She hoped they hadn't lost their chance to see if love led to more.

♥♥♥

Parker didn't know what to do with the new information about Ms. Passion beyond *something*. When Fiona got a call, he tried to use the break to take a step back from the situation and realign his brain.

"It's for you." She handed him the phone. "Chloe."

He was only mildly surprised. The FBI had *all* his electronics, so he'd put in a request to miss a few more days of competition filming, and included Fiona's number if there were any questions. "Hello," he said.

"You really know how to push the limits of good faith and a working relationship."

Parker was startled by the edge in Chloe's words. He had so many other things to worry about, though. "I followed the processes laid out in the rules, to notify of a lapse in coverage."

"Just because we don't have an elimination round this month doesn't mean you can go off and stop doing what you signed up for. You realize this is supposed to be a year commitment?"

He definitely wasn't in the mood for this. "I don't have any cameras. Fiona might as well be under house arrest—"

"Fiona. Not you. Replacing broken or lost equipment is part of the contract. I get it. This is an unusual situation. The issue is you weren't making quota before it happened. I can't make exceptions for you that no one else has access to."

"So boot me." Panic and a general sense of *what the fuck am I doing* spilled through him. But when his brain caught up, relief smothered the doubt.

Chloe's sigh was loud. "I'd like to think you're being sarcastic, but I don't even know anymore."

Did he mean it? A voice screamed in his head to stop, apologize, and beg for a chance to make things right. And the notion soured in his gut. "I'm being serious. In fact, consider this my resignation."

"You have to follow the rules for that, too. And I'm going to remind you that dropping out early means you lose access to any monetization options from us for the next year."

That would hurt. Not as much as some things, but it would leave a dent in his wallet. And he'd been struggling with revenue before this whole thing started. But he'd also set out on this journey to do what he enjoyed. If that wasn't happening anymore, he was better off taking a normal job. If it came down to it. "I understand. I'll issue my resignation video this afternoon, and you'll have my notice in writing shortly thereafter."

"What happened to *all my equipment was confiscated?*"

"I'll use Fiona's phone."

"All right." Chloe's voice was tight. "It'll will be a shame to lose you, but I understand. Best of luck in your future endeavors."

"Thanks." He disconnected, and turned back to face Fiona.

She was watching him with wide eyes. "I'd ask what that was, but I think I heard the important details."

"Yeah. It's done. I'm out of the competition." Each time he said it, it got easier.

Fiona's shock melted to a frown. "I'm sorry."

"Don't be. It's better this way."

He was free of the restraints and could go back to doing this the way he loved.

He had no idea how he'd handle the loss of

income. He'd have to surrender sponsorships he'd picked up for the competition. Quitting this way was the equivalent of cutting his paycheck down by three-quarters.

As the numbers rolled through his thoughts and reality sank in, the decision didn't feel so good after all. Had he made a huge mistake?

Chapter Twenty-Five

Wyatt was back in a questioning room, waiting for Agent Landry. He didn't suspect he'd be kept for hours this time. He'd opened his request with, "I'm ready to talk about everything. I'm waiving my right to have my attorney present."

He'd had days to think. An unoccupied brain could run off on a lot of tangents. One of the conclusions he arrived at was that he couldn't bullshit a bullshitter. Not that he'd been lying to Landry before, but he'd held cards close to his chest. Matched ego with ego.

Wyatt was going to take a page from Fiona's book and be honest. See how Landry reacted to that.

The door swung open, and Landry entered and took the seat across from him. The digital recorder went in the middle of the table, and he hit *Record.* "Repeat what you told the officer, on the record."

Wyatt met his gaze and didn't flinch. "I'll tell you everything I know. And I'm waving my right to have an attorney present." It might be the stupidest thing he'd done in a long time, but nothing else was working.

Besides, if Fiona could pull it off, there was something to it. He had serious respect for the way she held herself. Mimicking her couldn't be an all-bad idea.

"What do you want in return?" Landry asked. "Reduced sentence? Is this another plea bargain? You're familiar with those."

There was no reason to remind him Wyatt's past felony was off the record. "I want you to catch the person who actually did this. And I'd like to know how Fiona is."

"Of course you would. She's fine. In protective custody. Under round-the-clock guard. Away from harm's reach. How do you feel about that?"

Wyatt felt bad for Fiona. It had to be driving her nuts. "Pretty fucking relieved." He didn't try to mask the sincerity in the emotion. There was no reason to hide anything.

"Great. That's out of the way. What did you want to tell me?" Landry was a blank wall. That would change.

"I forgot—I have one other question." Wyatt leaned back in his seat, making himself as comfortable as was possible in shackles. "Do you think I'm stupid?"

Landry snorted. "No."

"But you think I flagrantly left evidence everywhere. Fingerprints. Bomb-making supplies…"

Landry's back was straight and his hands clasped in front of him. The same posture he'd worn since he sat. "I was hoping you'd tell me why."

"Because I didn't do it. But here's what I think you're doing. You arrested me in a flash. An investigation like this should take weeks or even months—"

"This isn't some television police procedural." Landry's tone was bland.

"Because something like this, the potential for a serial bomber, turns into big news fast. You found easy evidence, you were under pressure to make an arrest, so you built a shitty case around something handed to you, and hand-picked for relevance."

"*You* handed us the evidence. You were careless."

"Obsessed, right?" Wyatt wasn't bothered by the direction of the conversation. So far it was what he expected. But Landry was a reasonable man. Wyatt was banking on it. "That's the story you're going with?"

"Obsession fits your behavior."

Wyatt was willing to admit that was true. Another thing he'd had far too long to think about. Whether he'd crossed those lines Devin said were so blurry. He kept coming back to the same answer—consent. She was all right with it, and that changed the narrative. "I *am* obsessed with Fiona Walters."

Landry's fingers twitched, but he remained otherwise still. "The heart can make a person do strange things."

"I've gone out of my way to make sure she and I are in the same place, on a number of occasions, to catch her attention." Wyatt didn't think he'd be comfortable with this honesty thing, but there was a freedom in it.

Landry untangled his fingers.

"And Fiona knows what I've done," Wyatt said. He needed a chance to tell her more, though. To apologize. To tell her how he felt.

"So why the bombs?"

Wyatt raised his eyebrows. "You tell me."

"Clever."

Wyatt didn't care about the flat response. "When the first one went off, I was with Fiona. I'm not talking about *I cornered her and made her talk to me*. We were in an implementation meeting."

"No you weren't."

Had Wyatt flinched? What gave him away? It didn't matter. He should have stuck with the whole story. If Landry was this observant, maybe there was hope for Wyatt making his case. "That's what it says on my calendar. I was really fucking her on my desk." When Landry tapped the edge of the recorder, Wyatt added. "It was consensual."

"Says you."

"Says her. She'll confirm it. With her boyfriend in the room. I believe you've talked to Ms. Walters. Does she strike you as a dishonest person? An accomplished liar?"

"Where were you when the second bomb went off?" If Landry meant the shift to throw Wyatt off-balance, he was about to be disappointed.

"With Fiona again. And Parker."

"Convenient that only two people can corroborate any of your stories."

Wyatt narrowed his eyes. "The same two people I'm supposed to be stalking. The hotel security cameras saw us come in. Electronic locks will show me entering my room and that they didn't reach theirs until hours later. You can't pick and choose your circumstantial evidence."

Landry hesitated. That was new.

Wyatt latched onto it. "They're records I know you've got on file. That you subpoenaed them before you arrested me. Unless you were so anxious to make your case that you willfully ignored steps in the investigation."

"I don't tell you how to sell software." An edge crept into Landry's voice. "You have an accomplice, or Chicago wouldn't have happened. And the bombs weren't sent at the same time they detonated."

"Right. The mysterious accomplice. Who?" Wyatt had an opening now. This was what he needed and hadn't realized it.

"We're close to uncovering that."

"Sure you are."

"Give me a name, and it could help you."

Wyatt had played that game before. "Help me understand this. I'm good enough to hide my interactions with an accomplice to the point where you don't even have any suspects, but I left my fingerprints on a memory card with Fiona's picture on it."

"Obsession knows no reason." Landry had dropped the mask at this point.

"*Obsession*. My supposed motivation. Tell me again why I used bombs?"

"You were with her when they went off. She turned to you for comfort—"

"She turns to Parker for comfort." The words

tasted foul. "And why would it hit her that hard? It's tragic, and she's a sympathetic person, but why would that register any higher on her radar than any other tragic news? None of it impacted her directly until you involved her."

"Until *you* involved her, by leaving her information at each crime scene. Besides, those explosions might have gone off at the wrong time."

Wyatt was starting to see how this worked, and he didn't like the picture. Landry wasn't operating on facts. He'd already decided Wyatt was guilty, and was bending information to meet that expectation. "So I'm careless, stupid, incompetent, and enough of a mastermind to hide an accomplice, who I could have framed instead of being in here myself."

"You're not a bomb maker."

Exactly. Wyatt was running out of angles to attack this from. There wasn't enough logic for him to cling to.

"You can talk me in circles all day if you want," Landry said. "It doesn't change the evidence."

That should be Wyatt's line. "How does the rest of your story go, then? You find enough *clues*—flimsy or otherwise—to put me away. Or at least get me through a trial. You get all the praise and glory. Your bosses back off. Job well done. Anything that happens after, bombing related, you either blame it on this mysterious accomplice or on a copycat.

"If I'm as unhinged as you say, that I committed a crime to gain the attention of a woman who'd already noticed me, by blowing up boxes that had nothing to do with her, maybe my defense is insanity." Or maybe Landry's was.

Landry shrugged. "A hard thing to prove. You have to be tested by court doctors. You have to make the jury believe you're nuts, and not just intelligent and arrogant. Juries hate smart people, by the way."

Wyatt suspected they'd hate hearing how Landry was talking about them even more. "You're not making any sense."

"If you know your motives are fucked up, then you don't have much of a defense."

Wyatt didn't know what else to say. Logic wasn't winning out. The truth didn't do him any good. Reality seemed to be fragmented. This guy was a believer, and he'd put all his faith in Wyatt's guilt.

"Who's your accomplice?" Landry asked.

Wyatt was done trying to talk this through. Time to go back to the simple answers. "I don't have one. Because I didn't do anything."

"What do you want from Fiona Walters?"

"To spend the rest of my life with her." The opportunity to tell her exactly that.

"How does setting off a series of package bombs accomplish that?"

Wyatt raked his fingers through his hair. "I have no fucking idea."

Landry stood. "We're done here."

Apparently they were done before Wyatt had been brought in for questioning the first time around. How the fuck was he supposed to fight that?

Parker sat next to Fiona on a bench in the local courthouse. They'd asked her to come down and give a more formal deposition. If they were anywhere else, the officer accompanying them would look out of place. Like he did when they went out to dinner. Or sightseeing. Or anything.

Here, the man fit in.

Fiona bounced her leg at jackrabbit speed, and Parker rested his hand on her knee to calm her. She glanced at him with a faint smile and went back to staring off into space and fidgeting.

It had been almost a week since he quit the competition. He'd posted a few brief videos to his channel, to keep up with subscribers, but that was it. Not having the deadline and rules hanging over his head removed such a huge weight from his chest. The worries that came with his decision paled in comparison to his peace of mind.

"How much longer do you think we'll be waiting?" Fiona sounded as impatient and nervous as she looked.

Parker wished he could do more for her than *be here*. It felt like such a vague, ineffective thing.

The officer with them—John? Joe?—shrugged. "You know as much as me."

He'd already told them their odds were as good of getting in right away as they were of being stuck here for a few hours. It all depended on how long the person before them took.

Fiona stood. "I need to use the restroom. If they call my name before I'm back, tell them I waited two hours; they can hold on for five more minutes."

"Will do." Parker squeezed her hand.

As she walked away, the officer followed. She cast a glare at him. "It's around the corner, and we're in a courthouse, surrounded by people like you. I can walk there on my own."

The man didn't look fazed. "I'm sure you can. But I'll be outside the door."

Parker waited. As the minutes passed, his leg adopted the same bounce Fiona's had.

The officer returned alone and handed Parker his cell phone. "It's for you. Your sister. She says there's a family emergency and she told dispatch she needs to talk to you *now*. Make it quick."

Parker didn't have a sister. He took the phone. "Hello?"

The officer glanced over his shoulder every few seconds, as if Fiona might vanish into oblivion if he wasn't careful.

"You're a difficult guy to get a hold of." A woman's voice greeted him.

Fury spilled over Parker. It was Ms. Passion. "Might be because the FBI confiscated all of my electronics." The only reason he didn't hang up was that he wanted to ask her about her connection to Tim. Not that she would answer, but she was the one who placed the call. "What do you want?"

"Hear me out. You can keep hating me; you have every right. God, I'm so sorry."

He didn't care about the apology in her voice. "I'm listening, and then you can tell me about Greg and Tim."

"Gregory. Never Greg. That's why I'm calling. You know? Of course you do. That fucking wedding photo. You have no idea how furious their family was about what happened to Tim."

"*What happened to Tim?*" Parker spat her words back at her. "How about *what Tim did to*

Fiona? Any of them care about that?"

"You don't understand. I know the guy. He would never—"

"He did. I saw it. Why are you calling?" Parker had zero patience for this.

"The video I did, where I said Fiona was their suspect? Gregory gave me that information. Said he knew someone on the inside. He used to be in law enforcement, so he's got friends in unique places. He's my husband. Of course I believed him. Busting that story first, before anyone else knew? That would make my channel."

Sick and disgust churned inside Parker. "You were already *made*. You were willing to sell out a stranger for a couple more subscriptions?"

"I wasn't selling anyone out. Gregory assured me she was their suspect. I never would have said… I thought he was telling the truth. And he was furious when he found out they'd arrested someone else. He gets mad sometimes, but not like this. I was scared. Not that he'd hurt me. Never. But it was tense."

Parker clenched his free hand so tight, his knuckles ached. None of this was making him feel better. Now he wanted to find this Gregory guy and take another swing at him. The hits he landed in diner weren't nearly enough. "If you're looking for forgiveness, I don't have it for you."

"I'm not. I already told you that. Gregory left on business a few days ago. He travels a lot for work. no big deal. But this time, I was cleaning the garage and I found things. Camera equipment the same brand as I've seen in your videos. Supplies…"

"What kind of supplies?" Parker's gut

clenched, as he jumped to an answer without her saying the words.

"I didn't know at first. Wires. Batteries. Prepaid cell phones. But then I found pieces of a half-shredded printout. Bomb-making instructions. And I checked his cell phone GPS. It might be wrong, but it says he's in Chicago—"

Parker disconnected without listening to the rest, and shoved the phone back at Josh. "Where's Fiona?" he asked. It had been almost ten minutes. She should be back.

Josh shook his head. Parker sprinted past him and around the corner of the hallway. He paused for half a breath in front of the women's restroom, before pushing inside.

A brunette in front of the mirror looked at him with a raised eyebrow. "Get out, or I'll scream."

"Fiona?" Parker's question bounced off tile.

Nothing.

He looked at the woman. "Did you see a redhead in here?"

"No. Get the fuck out."

Parker stepped back into the hallway, to find Josh waiting. "Lock the building down," Parker said. "I think the bomber is here, and with Fiona."

Josh was already dialing. "You'd better feed me information as I ask for it," he said to Parker, before he put the phone to his ear.

Parker nodded and shot his gaze around the hallway. Was she in one of these rooms? Someplace else? Several minutes was a long time to get someplace new if no one was looking for you.

He couldn't believe this was happening again.

Chapter Twenty-Six

Fiona was surprised to walk out of the restroom and not find Officer Reynolds waiting. Parker's voice carried from around the corner, loud enough she heard the frustration, but not enough she knew what he was saying.

Something hard jammed into the small of her back, startling her, and a male voice said, "It's a gun, and I'd rather not shoot you but I will, so only make a scene if you plan on dying." His voice was low and steady, only meant for her ears. "Walk." His tone implied it wasn't a good idea to call his bluff.

Every muscle in her body coiled, until an ache ran from her neck to her feet. His demand and approach were cliché, but she wasn't in a position to point that out. With each step, her heart pounded louder, until she thought it might tear from her chest.

They climbed the stairs one floor, and he shoved her into a room halfway down the hallway. Why didn't they go further? A building sweep would find them in a few minutes.

She sure as fuck wasn't going to point that out to him.

She spun as he locked the door behind them, and wasn't surprised to see Gregory. Fiona refused to crack for this man. She wouldn't show him any fear. She wouldn't be the helpless maiden in distress she was when his brother forced her into his hotel room.

"Sit." He gestured to one of the chairs.

Her pulse hammered in her ears, but every sound and smell and sight was amplified. It was too bright. His voice and breathing were too loud. He reeked of body odor.

She'd find a way out. She wouldn't be a victim again. As the promises echoed in her head, determined the best way to rush him. Could she do it without getting shot? He was bigger than her. She know from his fight with Parker that he hit hard...

Gregory pointed the gun at his own head. "Now you listen, or I shoot myself." His tone was as unwavering as his grip.

Her breakfast surged into her throat, and she swallowed it back. "I'm listening."

"Why aren't you in jail?" he asked.

That was the last thing she expected to hear. Even, *Would you like a cup of coffee?* would make more sense. "Because I didn't do anything wrong?"

His laugh was sharp, slicing more of her composure. "That didn't matter with that Wyatt guy you let take your place. It sure as hell didn't make a difference for Tim."

"*Tim* stalked me, bound me, and threatened me. He locked me in a room against my will—" She cut off the words when Gregory thumbed back the hammer on his pistol.

"That memory card came from your boyfriend's laptop bag. The supplies were thrown away in your hotel garbage can. Why didn't the police arrest you?" Gregory's voice was low but terrifying.

Fiona's skin burned hot with panic. She forced herself to breathe, despite the fist closing around her lungs. "I don't know."

"Why the fuck are you still *free*?" He shouted the last word, and she jumped.

Was she supposed to answer him again? She tried to be subtle about surveying their surroundings. Not that there was much to see. A table in the middle of the room. The chair she sat in and one other. Would he really shoot himself? Would he hesitate if she rushed him?

Then what?

"Tim's a little odd, but you like weird and nerdy." Gregory stared at her, barely blinking. "All you had to do was hear him out. Give him a chance. Instead, you had to call the fucking police."

She didn't know what to say. She wouldn't apologize. Things weren't supposed to go like this. She'd been careful this time around. Kept her location private, her plans—everything. And she was still cornered by another psycho.

"Tell me more about Tim." She couldn't think of anything else to say, but keeping this guy talking seemed like a smart move.

She prayed no one burst into the room and startled him.

"You don't care."

"Of course I do." She gripped the truth of the statement. "He's a human being. I don't like to see people hurt. You know that, or you wouldn't be holding a gun to your own head."

"It's a waste of breath."

No. She had to make him go all mad-villain and explain his plan. Or anything that meant the conversation didn't stop. "He found me on YouTube, right?"

As she said the words, inspiration struck. Parker had used her phone to stream his last video. He was still logged into the app. What were the odds that she could start broadcasting?

Slim to none, especially using voice commands, but she was sure as fuck going to try. "Maybe he opened YouTube. During a recently started live stream." Who the fuck talked like that? Was she giving herself away? "To check out Maxine's competition—"

"Don't you dare bring her into this." Gregory spoke through clenched teeth. "You've ruined her career, too. How many more of the people I love do you think you're going to take down?"

"So you wanted to get back at me. I get that. I'd do a lot for my family. What was the plan?"

"I told you. Steal the memory card and business card covered in your fingerprints. Plant the supplies in your hotel room after you left. No one was going to get hurt. Just you."

He'd been in her hotel room. She thought she couldn't feel sicker. Apparently she was wrong. "How does that help Tim?"

"It doesn't, you fucking cunt. You already fucked him over. But at least you'd know what he was going through. He just wanted to get to know you. How hard would it have been to give him a chance?"

"I'm in a relationship." It was a weak response, but it was the safest thing she could think of that didn't compromise her opinion. Was now really the time to be stubborn about that?

Yes. God damn it. He wasn't taking her beliefs from her, even just vocally.

"With a media whore who fucked half the world before you. Tim would have treated you like a princess."

Princess Peach. The random thought sent a tremor of irrational amusement from her, and she swallowed a giggle. She was so tempted to ask about Maxine—Ms. Passion—and her channel, but she had no idea what this man wanted or what he was capable of.

"What now, then?" she asked. "You have me here, in a courthouse. At any moment, someone will find me. You know they're looking, right? I came here with a police escort. Then what?"

"I shoot myself." He made it sound like the most obvious answer. "You live with the guilt."

She nearly gagged on the thought. So much of this didn't make any sense. If this were a mystery movie, they'd have found him in the first act. There was no way she was helping this guy figure out the holes in his plan, though. "What about everyone else in your family? I'm not worth the stress this will put them under."

"You're the reason they're under stress." His shout made her eardrums throb.

Tears trickled down her cheeks, and her eyes stung. She didn't dare brush them away.

Her lungs were starting to burn too. She dragged in a deep breath, and nearly choked on the ache. What the fuck? Was this a panic attack? A heart attack?

Tears slid down Gregory's face, too. Was that regret?

"There has to be another way." Her throat felt raw.

"You know there's not. What the fuck is in the air?" He wiped the back of his hand across his face.

Was that it? Something in the vents? Her eyes itched now, begging for relief. She sat still. "Nothing, as far as I know. Are you all right?"

"Fuck. I'm fine. I'm just—" He wiped his cheeks again. His eyes were red and swollen.

The air smelled funny. Or was that stress? Her sinuses burned.

A loud *bang* cracked through the air, and Fiona swore her heart stopped. Did he shoot himself?

Chapter Twenty-Seven

"On the floor, now," someone shouted. Men in body armor and masks rushed into the room, and one tackled Gregory.

Fiona gasped, and her lungs protested. Her eyes watered enough that she struggled to make out what was happening.

"Room is secured," a different voice called. "We have them both."

A figure knelt next to her and pressed something cool and damp to her face. "Close your eyes," he said. "Hold this in place and don't rub. We have an ambulance waiting."

She nodded. Her words were gone. She wanted to sink back onto the floor and cry.

"Come on." Someone helped her to her feet. "Lean on me. I won't let you fall. You can lose your shit in about two minutes, after we wipe away the traces of tear gas. Okay?"

"Okay." Her own voice sounded distant.

♥ ♥ ♥

Two hours later, Fiona sat the edge of an examination table in the emergency room, waiting for the police to find her, so she could answer their questions and be discharged. One of the agents on the bombing case had alerts turned on for Parker's channel, so when Fiona activated the live stream—she still couldn't believe that worked—the talking gave police enough information to know how to approach the room.

They'd evacuated the building quickly, since bombs might be involved, shut off the HVAC, and let enough pepper spray into the room to make breathing uncomfortable.

She didn't know the logistics of decontamination, but she was grateful their plan worked.

Parker had refused to leave her side, though he wasn't allowed to touch her until the contaminated clothes came off. A nurse finally convinced him that, while Fiona was in the shower, he should go buy her a T-shirt and sweats from the gift shop, so she wouldn't have to go home in a hospital robe.

He looked smug when he handed her the plastic bag. The shirt he found said *Bad Ass Chick* and had a cartoon baby duck on it.

"I don't know what's worse—that the shop sells this or that you thought it was funny." Fiona was smiling, though. The terror wasn't the same as last time. She felt like she'd played a part in freeing herself.

Maybe not a big one, but he hadn't taken her

power.

Parker slid between her legs and wrapped his arms around her waist. "You look good. Does the rest matter?"

"You're so very biased."

"I'm so very right." He kissed the tip of her nose.

The sound of a throat clearing drew her attention to an officer standing in the doorway. "Ms. Walters, I just need to get a statement from you, and a couple more pieces of information."

"And then I can go?"

"With an escort, until we're convinced that everything is cleared up."

She rolled her eyes. But the escort was only temporary. "All right. Ask away."

♥♥♥

As he changed into his street clothes, Wyatt listened to Fiona's conversation with Gregory. Charles had gotten him the recording, and it was Wyatt's third time through.

He would have liked an apology when they released him, but he wasn't surprised to not get one. He'd comfort himself with the knowledge that this probably ruined Landry's day, and would be happy Gregory's arrest should bring a stop to the bombings.

Everything he'd brought on this trip was in evidence, besides what he was wearing. He was assured that, once the paperwork was filled out, he'd get the rest of his belongings back. He could take it or leave it. He'd be hopping a plane back home, anyway, as soon as he could get a reasonably priced ticket.

Charles's fee had eaten into some of his savings, but not as much as it could have. Wyatt had a few months to find new work.

Hopefully, that would be enough time for people to forget his face and move on to the next big story.

He finished signing out of the police station, and walked toward the exit. He'd call an Uber to take him to a nearby hotel.

And he had no idea how he should reach out to Fiona. That kind of doubt was foreign to him.

He pushed outside and paused, letting the sun hit his face and the cool autumn air brush his skin.

"Hey, handsome. Need a ride?" Parker's question came from behind.

Wyatt felt his first genuine smile in days. It stretched his cheeks more than the news he was being released. He turned toward the greeting, to find Fiona and Parker waiting near the building, a few feet from the door. Wyatt approached the pair, his mind leaping along possibilities. Apologizing. Devouring Fiona. Just holding her and enjoying the company.

Fiona met him halfway and stopped him with her arm outstretched and her palm flat on his chest.

He opened his mouth to say something.

"Don't." Her tone was neutral. "Don't touch me. Don't say a word. Because if you're going to tell me you don't want to see me, if you're going to push me away or feed me a weak excuse about why we won't work, if you're going to lie to me, I'll leave. We'll call it *end of story*."

He kept his mouth shut, surprised and pleased

at her insistence.

"Well?" she asked.

"You told me not to say a word."

Parker snorted.

Fiona rolled her eyes but couldn't hide her threatening smile. "You can talk now."

Wyatt grasped her wrist loosely, earning a gasp that drove to his every nerve ending. He held her gaze. "I'm not planning on leaving or asking you to leave ever again." Maybe he should have planned more than just *tell her how you feel*, but he didn't expect to see her yet. The words felt right, regardless. "I'll stay by your side for as long as you'll have me. You haunt my thoughts and dreams, and I don't want that to ever stop. I've made a lot of mistakes recently, but coming back to you—both of you—again and again, is the one thing I've done right. I love you. Mind, body, and soul."

The way she bit her lip was like the faintest tease of a good drug. "You probably already know this, but so it's out there, I'm not leaving Parker. You have to share."

"I want you to stay with him. The two of you together are serendipity. I won't displace him any more than he will me." Wyatt's words earned him another smirk from Parker. "But I do want an equal place in your heart."

"You still have some trust to earn, though you've made up for a lot." Fiona's arm went slack, the weight of her wrist resting against his palm.

"That's fair. Give me the chance, and I'll prove myself." He hadn't missed that she didn't return those three little words, but he could give her time.

"I want you. I need you. Unless you tell me to fuck off, I'll do everything in my power to add my name to your equation."

Fiona's smile broke through. "I like the sound of that."

"You'd better," Parker said. "You've been pushing pretty hard for it."

She glanced over her shoulder. "Not *that* hard."

Wyatt had missed this as much as anything. The easy banter. That Parker and Fiona didn't have an issue doing this in front of a police station. "There's a joke in there, but it's too easy."

"Something about this relationship should be." Parker's tone was light.

Fiona lightly tapped Wyatt's chest. "You can kiss me now," she said.

"I have your permission?"

"Consider it granted indefinitely, until otherwise revoked."

Wyatt tightened his grip on her wrist, pulled her in, and moved his free hand to the base of her neck, capturing her. He crushed his mouth to hers, letting everything he felt flow through the kiss. Hunger. Need. Desire. Love. Adoration.

She gripped his shirt and pressed closer. The full-body contact sang through him. He let go of her, to glide his hands down and cup her ass. She tasted like coffee and promises, and smelled like springtime.

He dragged his lips along her jaw and up to her ear. "*Fuck*, I missed this," he murmured against her skin.

Her giggle vanished in a sigh. "It hasn't even

been two weeks."

"Entirely too long for my taste."

"Are we doing this right here and now?" Parker asked. "In front of the police station? That's a serious question, by the way. I'm down for whatever, as long as it doesn't land anyone back in jail."

Wyatt broke away but wasn't ready to let go of Fiona. "Believe it or not, I'm not up for anything quite so risky. Not yet."

"Prison sate all your needs?" Fiona teased.

"I will slap your ass for that." If he could release her long enough to get a good angle. "Before I do anything else, I want a real shower, a comfortable place to sit, and food not purchased on the state's budget."

Parker gestured to the parking lot. "Car's over there. Our hotel room has a king-sized bed and nonstop hot water. It's good for more than just fucking, if you're into other things."

"Keep in mind, we'll be offended if you planned to stay somewhere else." Fiona nudged him toward the parking lot.

He followed without protest. "Never even considered it. How rude would I be, turning down such a generous offer?"

When they reached the hotel, Parker loaned Wyatt a shirt and a pair of shorts. Wyatt could figure out a better clothing solution tomorrow. It was odd being this casual around anyone, but with these two, it felt right.

He excused himself, to shower. Experience said he needed to take the opportunity now, to invite Fiona to join him. Reason argued that she'd still be here after, and in the morning. Tonight, he wanted to focus on the relationship at the intellectual and emotional level. Or, if he was using more direct words, movies, pizza, and cuddling.

Wyatt took his time, letting the hot water rinse his tension away. There was no pressure to be anywhere else. Nothing looming that couldn't wait another day.

He liked it.

He finished his shower, toweled off, and dressed. The borrowed clothes were tighter than he preferred. Another foreign feeling to add to the list—stepping from the bathroom and being exposed. Not physically, but as himself. There were no masks in here.

Fiona grinned when she saw him and patted the mattress next to her. "Saved you a spot."

It looked perfect. He made himself comfortable. She was leaned against Parker on her other side, but she rested a hand on Wyatt's leg, tracing tiny lines with her thumb. It was cozy.

They ordered takeout. Watched whatever was on HBO and currently playing. Made jokes and recited the memorable lines along with the actors. Stayed up way too late, drifting closer toward sleep, until they all succumbed. It was perfect.

He woke up the next morning, to find Fiona watching him, sleep lingering in her green eyes. He tucked a strand of red hair behind her ear. "A guy could get used to this."

"Being watched while you sleep?" Her tone was playful.

"Waking up to the sound of your girlfriend

flirting with someone else?" Parker grumbled.

Fiona reached behind her and swatted. "Grump."

"It's early. If you're both morning people, I want to change my answer in regard to all of this." The sleep was fading from his voice.

Fiona laughed. It was an incredible sound. "Too late. No takebacks."

Being pressed this close to her, the heat of her body searing through thin clothes, drew Wyatt the rest of the way to consciousness. Last night was about reconnecting, but this morning, his body was eager for more. "What about you? Any desire for takebacks?"

"Just one." Her brief reply dampened his mood. "And I guess it's not really a takeback so much as a do-over. I've wanted to say this for a while, and I've felt it for even longer, but *God*, you make things difficult sometimes with your posturing and pushing away and pretending you don't care—"

"Red," Parker interrupted. "Make your point, so we can fuck then go get breakfast."

Wyatt laughed. This was what he was in for by sticking around, and he loved it.

A blush spread across Fiona's face, and she bit her bottom lip. "*My point is*, I love you too. As much as I love Parker. You hold equal but distinctly separate places in my heart, and I'm glad I don't have to get over you."

The words made Wyatt's heart swell. He'd never thought hearing them would mean so much, but her *I love you* was worth more than the biggest promotion or raise. He traced a finger along her bottom lip, tugging it free. "Yeah?"

"Absolutely." She drew his finger into her mouth and sucked.

The sensuality tugged an invisible cord that ran straight to his cock, and he groaned.

Wyatt gripped the back of her neck, needing to taste those full, pouty lips. He kissed her hard, holding her captive.

Fiona's body molded to his. It was a perfect fit. This reality, the sounds and smells—all of it—was so much better than his memory insisted.

Parker glided a hand up Fiona's stomach, between her and Wyatt, to cup her breast and pinch her nipple. His knuckles dug into Wyatt's chest. The hard scrape against her soft form was a new kind of enticing.

Wyatt slid his hand down her back, to cup her ass. He pulled her tighter against him. "We have a problem," he said. His erection dug into her stomach and twitched at the contact.

She pouted, but a smile threatened underneath. "What kind of problem?"

"I don't like having one arm restrained."

Parker snorted a laugh.

Fiona's grin broke through. "But it's okay in my case?"

Wyatt kissed her again, catching her bottom lip between his teeth when he pulled away. "You tell me." He gripped her hip and nudged. "I want to watch you ride me."

"Yes, sir." She straddled his legs when he rolled onto his back.

He could feel her heat through her panties and

his boxers, taunting him. Maybe he should have thought this through better and removed some clothes before they got to this point.

She pressed her soft mound into him, grinding against his cock, as she rocked her hips in a slow sway.

Then again, that felt fucking incredible, and it might be the only way to draw out the moment without blowing his wad too soon.

The mattress shifted. Out of the corner of his eye, Wyatt saw Parker kneel, work his dick free, and stroke as he watched.

Being on display was another layer of arousal, overriding Wyatt's desire to draw things out. He grabbed Fiona's thighs, digging his thumbs into the flesh, to stop her. He pushed her back enough to tug down the waist of his boxers, then nudged aside the crotch of her panties, to slide inside her.

God, she felt good. He let out a long groan as she wrapped around him, slick and tight and warm. The silent parting of her lips sparked all his nerve endings to life.

Wyatt wanted everything at once. A hard, fast fuck. Something slow and teasing. To make Fiona moan. Scream. Beg. To push her to the edge of pleasure and keep her there for as long as possible.

Rent stupid movies. See the world. Learn how she liked her coffee. Tie her up. Pin her down. Watch her with Parker.

There was time for all of that, and he was looking forward to every single minute.

Chapter Thirty-Eight

Fiona's body hummed with anticipation.

There was an intimacy in this moment. It was more than sex. Sure, there was that physical need to be closer to Wyatt. The thrill that came from Parker watching.

But there was an underlying connection that heightened her senses.

Wyatt drew his fingers up her spine in a deceptively light touch, and pulled her into him. He pumped his hips, setting a slow and steady pace inside her.

He laid a trail of kisses, from her mouth down to her chin and along her neck, then bit her shoulder. She whimpered at the sharp sting. Her awareness cranked up another notch. She swore she could feel *everything*.

When he moved his hand to her breast and rolled a nipple between his fingers, she clenched her pussy around him. The whispers of pain added a delicious edge to the pleasure, like salty mixed with sweet.

She arched her back in surprise when Parker traced a slippery finger along the crack of her ass.

The new contact was more of a shock because the lube was still cold, but it heated quickly on her skin. They'd played around a bit with anal, but with so much anticipation building inside her, this promise jumbled her thoughts.

Parker teased her puckered hole with his finger. She wanted more but didn't know if she had enough grasp of her vocal chords to ask.

Wyatt glided his hands to her ass and spread her cheeks.

Parker nudged her tight opening with the head of his cock, and time slowed to a crawl. He slid inside her. An inch at a time, then waiting for her to relax and be ready.

"You okay?" Parker asked, his breath hot on her ear.

"Yes." She licked her lips and swallowed at the raspy response, trying to work more moisture back into her mouth.

There was no rocking, but when he was buried completely inside her, she felt like she could breathe again. The double penetration stretched her in a new way. It was almost too much, but it felt so good.

Parker reached around and sought out her clit. There was no thrusting. No other movement. Just his stroking the sensitive button, while Wyatt sucked and bit her neck.

Climax came from nowhere, rushing in and spilling inside. She didn't know which way to bend or arch to feel everything. Her head was filled with helium, threatening to float away. This was incredible.

While she was still wrapped in the high, Wyatt gripped her thighs and set a slow, steady pace. Parker matched his rhythm, sliding her back and forth between them, trapping her in a delicious push and pull.

Parker moved his touch from her tender core to grab her hips. The way she was pressed between them, each thrust rubbed against her clit.

Another orgasm built inside, heightened by the sensations and the sounds of the men on either side of her. Wyatt's grunts mingled with Parker's groans in a delicious chorus.

When she came again, the orgasm was drawn out, rather than abrupt. It stole her thoughts and kept her in the clouds in her head.

There was too much stimulus for her to name each feeling, so she stopped trying to focus on any one thing. She let herself fall into everything at once, as they enveloped her.

She was vaguely aware of Parker—his pace increasing, the way he hammered hard against her, and the delicious, familiar sound of his climax.

Wyatt sank his teeth into her neck and his fingers into her thighs. His grunts had teased her dreams, but awake, with him here, they were so much more potent. She recognized the sound of him coming as well.

As everyone slowed to a stop, she emerged from the space in her head, but not completely. She collapsed on Wyatt's chest and listened to the hammering of his heart.

The only sounds in the room were heavy breathing and the air conditioner. Wyatt's skin was damp with exertion, and Fiona suspected hers was as well.

This was so perfect. Not just the sex, though she wouldn't surrender that for anything, but the union. This bond between both men that meant the world to her.

Parker slipped out of her, leaving her body feeling both empty and relieved. He laid a soft row of kisses down her back.

No one spoke, but they didn't need to. They were all thinking and feeling similar things.

Wyatt trailed his fingers through her hair and lifted his head to kiss the top of hers.

Life with Parker was damn near perfect, in all the ways that mattered. She would have been happy with just him for the rest of her life.

But this was *more*. She didn't want to imagine the future without Wyatt, any more than she could picture Parker not being there.

And she wouldn't have it any other way.

Parker had spent so much of his adult life looking for this. It had always been so vague and out of reach, he hadn't been able to name it, let alone grasp it.

When he asked Fiona to join him for the competition, he hoped she'd be the answer. Instead, this feeling of contentment and belonging was both far easier and much more complicated to find.

Now he strolled through a random small town,

down a Main Street that could be fifty years old or a hundred, with Fiona and Wyatt. Parker was filming, not because he was on a schedule, but because he enjoyed seeing the world through his own eyes and the camera's lens at the same time.

Wyatt had given them a brief run-down of what happened here after they left. His story consisted of, *I was picked up, tossed in a cell, and no one believed I was innocent, so I stared at the wall a lot.*

It wasn't quite *opening up*, but it was a starting point. Now Wyatt was grilling Fiona on what happened in Chicago. The drive, the city, the protective custody… All of it.

Parker tuned most of it out. He'd lived it, and it was more enjoyable to watch Fiona's expression as it shifted from laughing to thoughtful. He didn't care for the way she surveyed everything around her, as though she was waiting for someone to jump out, but he didn't blame her. He did the same.

She looked happy, though. He didn't doubt she would have been content if it was only the two of them, but with Wyatt here, things felt complete.

A frown crossed her face, and she pursed her lips, then looked at Parker, as if waiting for an answer.

He shook the rambling observations aside. "I'm sorry—what?"

"Mr. Big Bad Wolf is going to abandon us and go back to Atlanta." Her pout was exaggerated, and amusement hid in her gaze.

Wyatt gave a heavy sigh. "It's where home is."

"And home is in Salt Lake for me," Fiona said. "You don't see me running off, based on such a weak excuse.”

It was easy for Parker to fall into this. “What happened to staying by her side?”

Wyatt paused in his walking and turned to face Parker. “Unlike some people, I didn’t make this trip intending to be on the road for an undetermined amount of time. I’m unwillingly unemployed. I need to sort at least a couple of things out in person. And no one said the two of you couldn’t join me.”

“You should have said so in the first place.” Parker liked the plan.

Fiona studied him as if he’d spoken a foreign language. “You hated Atlanta last time we were there. You couldn’t wait to leave.”

“True. But it was because I was trying to mold my life to that stupid competition. Besides, I was thinking of taking one of your suggestions for the show and tweaking it a little.” Now seemed like the perfect time to bring up the glimmer of a thought he’d tried and failed to ignore. “Best places around the world to fuck.” Hearing the words aloud made him hesitate. “It might need a more content-filter-friendly name.”

Fiona laughed. “It just might.”

“And I have the sexiest co-star ever,” Parker said.

She nodded at Wyatt. “Him?”

Parker grasped her fingers, held his camera arm to the side, and tugged her in, to brush his lips over hers. “You.”

“Nope. Not going to happen.” The playfulness vanished from Wyatt’s voice.

Fiona whirled to face him. “Excuse me?”

Wyatt wrapped an arm around her waist, turned her back—to face Parker—and kissed along the back of her neck. "After everything you've been through, you're going to stick yourself on camera again? No."

"That's not your choice." She pulled away. Her tone was still light, but it held a warning edge. "Staying in the shadows didn't work." She and Parker had talked about this. "I had a lot of fun. I won't stop looking over my shoulder, possibly ever, but I'm done planning my life around someone else's neurosis."

"You've already decided." Wyatt's expression was unreadable.

She nodded.

"Then I yield."

Her smile was back. "Good. Because we want you to join us."

"On camera?"

"Sure," Parker said. "No more clauses to worry about, with work."

Wyatt didn't look convinced. "Until the next place has a similar clause."

"So you negotiate it out of your contract. That's what you do, right?"

They stepped aside, as a couple pushing a baby in a stroller brushed past. Wyatt was uncharacteristically quiet.

"You can say *no*," Fiona told him.

"I could. The two of you have this chemistry on screen. I'd hate to disrupt it." As if wanting to prove his point, he took Parker's camera and moved so Parker and Fiona were in the shot.

Parker took the device back. "That never

stopped you before."

"Good point. It won't stop me now, either. I'm in."

Parker couldn't help his grin. This was definitely what he'd been looking for. What he was missing.

He could figure out the cash-flow situation, especially if they all bumped their heads together. Diversification in his revenue sources. New sponsorships.

Parker started this journey with nothing, and now he had more than he'd ever wished for. The rest would fall into place with a little work, and he was good with that.

Chapter Twenty-Nine

Fiona struggled to sit still. Every time her knee bounced without her permission, Wyatt squeezed her leg.

They were in a local coffee shop, a few blocks from his old corporate offices.

Nick was in town, to try to fix the contract issue with the shipping company, and he was meeting Fiona to come up with a game plan.

He didn't know about Wyatt, who'd assured Fiona this was the perfect time to tell her brother about Wyatt's long-term addition to her love life.

Fiona had some serious doubts, but Wyatt promised the conversation would be worth it, if Nick would hear him out.

She was trusting him—something that got less scary each time it worked out. It was true, it had only been a week since Wyatt was officially part of her and Parker's lives, but it had been an incredible week.

"You've got to be fucking kidding me." That

was Nick. He made eye contact with Fiona, then turned toward the door.

Wyatt gave her one more squeeze, and she sprinted after her brother.

She grabbed Nick's arm. "Stay long enough to hear us out."

"Where's Parker? You didn't dump him for this assmunch, did you?"

This was going about as well as Fiona expected. "He's negotiating a sponsorship with Milton Hotels. He was lucky to get on their calendar, so I told him we'd be fine without him. Come talk to us, please?"

"No." Nick looked past her, in Wyatt's direction. "I can't believe after everything we've gone through—"

"Stop. You encouraged me to do this thing with Parker, to have fun. To find myself. And I did, and I'm working on it. Wyatt is part of that equation. You *know* this company means as much to me as it does to you. Sit. Talk. Give us fifteen minutes, and please don't play the *him or your family* card, because I don't want to spend my life resenting you."

Nick scowled, but he followed her back to the table. Wyatt stood as they approached, and extended his hand.

Her brother shook it, but the gesture looked mechanical. They all sat again, and Wyatt tangled his fingers with Fiona's.

Nick's scowl deepened. "I'm not listening to anything he has to say, so I hope you're the one doing the talking," he said to Fiona.

"To start." She slid him a paper cup. "Large latte, extra shot, splash of cinnamon."

"Bribery won't help." Nick sipped the drink anyway.

Fiona steeled herself, to say what came next. Not because she doubted the words, but people tended to throw them around carelessly, and she needed Nick to believe her when she said it. "We're in love. Wyatt and I."

"What about Parker?"

If the situation were different, she'd ask Nick, *If you're so worried about Parker, why don't you date him?* Instead she said, "I love him too. And he's heard all of this. I'm not here to let you try to change my mind. That's not an option."

"I don't care who you're screwing or what you call the relationship." Nick's voice rose. He ducked his head when a few people at nearby tables looked in their direction. "As long as they're treating you right. Forgive me if I have a hard time believing that's the case here. This man fucked us over."

"No, he didn't," Fiona said. Wyatt set out to do that, but he hadn't needed to, and he'd proven to her satisfaction that he regretted misleading her. "I did that. Don't blame my mistakes on anyone but me. I chose to see him again. I chose not to disclose it."

Nick clenched his jaw, not speaking for a moment. "Call it what you want. It doesn't change the situation any."

"No, but I can," Wyatt said.

Fiona muttered a brief prayer that this went the way Wyatt predicted. "Hear him out?" she asked Nick.

"Nope. Not listening. Not interested. Nothing he can say will change my mind."

"I can tell you how to stop a lawsuit from the shipping company. You can end this today and have them sign an agreement that promises things are over." There was no doubt in Wyatt's voice.

Nick glared at him. "I'm still not listening. Do you tell me next that you'll go with me? Bullshit your way back into an office that will probably have security escort you out the moment you step foot on their property?"

"Nope. I'm going to tell you how to do the bullshitting, and you'll handle it." Despite Wyatt's smooth tone, his grip on Fiona's fingers tightened.

It was a tiny gesture. No one would see. But it told her he was taking this seriously, and was as nervous as she was.

"I haven't heard any good jokes lately. Do tell." Nick settled back in his seat with his drink.

Wyatt leaned in and rested his forearms on the table. "You'll meet with them, like planned. You'll ask that everyone drop the matter and move on. It will be more of a statement than a request. Tell them you'd like to keep the deposit—you've already done some work and it's fair to compensate you for your time. Recommend they call the situation even and that all parties sign a new agreement, closing this matter for good."

Nick let out a barking laugh. "Are you going to teach me how to do Jedi mind tricks? Because that's the only way I see that working. You talk a good game, but *God*, I hope you're not pulling this bullshit with my sister."

"He's serious, and he's got a way," Fiona said. "And it won't be bullshit."

"Right. Might as well get to the punchline, if that wasn't it." Despite the words, curiosity was replacing doubt in Nick's voice.

Wyatt's smile was grim. "I won't give you the details of what I know, unless you really want them. But what you do is remind them I wasn't involved in the sale process, and I didn't recommend they investigate your product or have any input on whether or not they purchased it."

"Pretty sure they already know that." Nick set down his cup and leaned in.

Fiona took that as a sign he was finally paying attention.

"You'll remind them anyway. And then you'll point out that you and I are on speaking terms—you probably want to practice so you can make it believable—and that I have a *very* good grasp on what is and isn't covered by my non-disclosure agreement, as it relates to my old job."

"You want me to threaten them?" Nick didn't sound as disgusted as Fiona had expected.

Wyatt shook his head. "I want you to remind them that *I* can threaten them."

"I won't blackmail my way out of this," Nick said.

"No, you won't. You don't have to make any threats. Like I said, you never have to hear the details. Tell them what I said you should, and walk away unsullied."

Fiona would dig deeper one day soon, and find out what Wyatt knew about their contracts that let him speak with this kind of confidence, but for today, she was sticking with not knowing, for the sake of plausible deniability.

"If they call my bluff?" Nick's question told her he was considering this seriously but making sure his bases were covered.

"It's up to you what you say next, but between you and me, I'll burn their company to the ground in a legal firestorm, to stop them from destroying yours. I know enough to do it. And it won't be for you; it will be for Fiona." Wyatt's voice had gone hard.

Goosebumps raced over her skin.

Nick was silent again, but the animosity was gone from his expression, and his posture relaxed. "You make a really solid pitch."

"It's not a *pitch*, and I don't care if you believe that, as long as you do something with what I've given you."

Fiona heard the shift in his tone. Wyatt was done negotiating. She wouldn't forgive either of them if they made her choose, but it wouldn't come down to that. Nick was stubborn, but he was rational.

Nick sighed. "I'll do what you said, and thank you for the information. But keep in mind that, if you hurt Fiona—"

"You'll what?" Wyatt asked. "The last two men who hurt her are in jail, and I'm not looking forward to going back any time soon. But tasteless jokes aside, I'm not planning on it. And if things don't work out—God forbid—that's between her and me."

It wasn't just the words that warmed Fiona. The firmness and certainty in Wyatt's response sent a pleasant glow spreading through her.

Nick *tsk*ed, a half-smile tugging up the corner of his mouth. "I'm out of counterarguments. And praying to anyone listening that things go even half as smoothly as you seem to think they will. But I'm not welcoming you to the family."

Wyatt grinned. "You will. But I have time."

"I do have one request." Nick turned to Fiona.

She couldn't begin to guess what it would be, after all that. "All right?"

"Please tell me I can start scheduling you for work again soon. I'm falling apart without my head programmer."

That made her smile. "Tomorrow. You can put me back on the schedule right away." Life really was all right. Back to normal. No. That wasn't quite right. Life was anything but ordinary, plus one, and she didn't want it any other way.

♥♥♥

Nick walked from the shipping-company building, his gait even despite his racing thoughts. He was stunned he'd kept his composure through that entire meeting, but was even more shocked about the fact that things went almost exactly as Wyatt predicted.

Nick hadn't used quite the same language, but he'd requested the matter be dropped and mentioned he'd spoken to Wyatt about the best way to approach a lawyer over arbitration.

That was enough to earn Nick a promise that the contract would be canceled without prejudice.

Someday, Nick might ask Wyatt what the actual threat was, but today he was happy to be free of the threat of legal repercussion.

He settled into his rental car, let his phone

connect, and cranked the stereo. Heavy bass and electric guitar blared from the stereo.

He pulled into traffic and navigated to the nearest strip mall, to find an empty parking spot at the edge of the lot.

Certain no one from the office could see him here, he shouted, "*Yes.*" The yell mingled with the music. He could let his composure slip here.

Nick still didn't understand what Fiona was up to with this *relationship* of hers. She and Parker had been all but a couple for as long as Nick could remember. He had no idea how Wyatt fit into that.

But he trusted Fiona. Not just because she was his sister, but she was his business partner for a reason.

The music vanished, and before he could process the abrupt silence, a loud ring jangled in his ears, startling him. The number was unfamiliar, but it was a Utah area code. He turned down the volume and hit *Answer* on his phone. "This is Nick Walters."

"Nick, hey. Scott McAllister. You have a minute?"

From Rinslet. Nick and Fiona's biggest business partner. "I've got as many as you need." Unless Scott was calling to cancel the contract. Nick suspected he wouldn't have access to any loopholes disguised as thinly-veiled threats in that case.

"Perfect. Is your passport current?"

"It could be."

"Awesome," Scott said. "Here's the thing—we have a contestant in Italy, a tattoo artist, and she needs some help managing contracts."

This was taking some getting used to. Nick

appreciated the infusion of cash they'd seen from the Rinslet deal, but it was odd, taking *suggestions* from the other company. "I can send Fiona." She'd love the excuse to get out of the country.

"You might want to keep her Stateside. Or rather, you probably want to handle this yourself."

Nick frowned at the steering wheel. "For a basic one-off software install?"

"For dealing with an heiress."

"I'm sorry—what?" Nick knew the contestant Scott was talking about. He'd familiarized himself with all of them, and Tara did stunning inkwork, most of it her original creations.

"The stuff no one discloses in the bios. Her family owns one of the largest tech companies in the country. I thought you might want to extend your reach a little. Fiona's brilliant, but she's not your negotiator, you are."

The possibilities avalanched in Nick's head. "Yeah. Absolutely. I'm all over that. Thank you."

"Gotta protect my investment." Scott chuckled.

Nick didn't care what Scott's reasons were, if it all worked out. He disconnected, already building a new plan in his head. He'd need someone to work sales here, if he was on the other side of the world, schmoozing a new potential partner.

He'd need a second person in the position anyway. So far, he was the only one pounding the pavement besides Fiona. He'd spent most of their new funds on developers, since it was a tech company. And he needed Fiona focused on that, not trying to negotiate deals, when she didn't like handling that side of the business.

He took a deep breath and dialed her number.

"Hey, you." Fiona sounded hesitant when she answered. "How'd it go?"

Right. The negotiation. That was already several steps behind him. "Good. Great. Exactly like Wyatt said it would."

"Yay." Her quick chirp brightened his mood further. "So we're in the clear."

"Yes. And I have another favor to ask." He couldn't believe he was about to do this.

"Sure. What's up?"

Was this a good idea? Nick could interview people. Salesmen were a dime a dozen. Good ones were a little harder to find, though. He didn't have time to train someone, but he could hire the right person and get them up to speed quickly.

Nobody who'd be willing to go to war to keep the business alive, though. "When you say you trust Wyatt, do you mean it?" he asked. "And I mean one-hundred percent, you put him on the same level as Parker?"

"Yes." She didn't hesitate.

"I don't suppose he'd be interested in working for us?"

THE END